Wild Spirit Revival

Montana Becketts ♦ Wild Spirit Ranch, Book One

Historical Western Romance

SHIRLEEN DAVIES

Book Series by Shirleen Davies

Historical Western Romances
Redemption Mountain
MacLarens of Fire Mountain Historical
MacLarens of Boundary Mountain
Montana Becketts ♦ Wild Spirit Ranch

Contemporary Western Romance
Cowboys of Whistle Rock Ranch
MacLarens of Fire Mountain Contemporary
Macklins of Whiskey Bend

Romantic Suspense
Eternal Brethren Military Romantic Suspense
Peregrine Bay Romantic Suspense

Find all my books at:
https://shirleendavies.com/books/
The best way to stay in touch is to subscribe to my newsletter. Go to my Website,
www.shirleendavies.com, and fill in your email and name in the
Join My Newsletter boxes.
That's it!

Copyright © 2024 by Shirleen Davies
Paperback Edition

All rights reserved. No part of this publication may be reproduced, distributed, or transmitted in any form or by any electronic or mechanical means, including information storage and retrieval systems or transmitted in any form or by any means without the prior written permission of the publisher, except by a reviewer who may quote brief passages in a review. No AI Training. Without in any way limiting the author's exclusive rights under copyright, any use of this publication to 'train' artificial intelligence (AI) technologies to generate text is expressly prohibited. The author reserves all rights to license uses of this work for generative AI training and development of machine learning language models. Thank you for respecting the hard work of this author.

> For permission requests, contact the publisher.
> Avalanche Ranch Press, LLC
> PO Box 12618
> Prescott, AZ 86304

Wild Spirit Revival is a work of fiction. Names, characters, places, and incidents are either products of the author's imagination or used fictitiously. Any resemblance to actual events,

Cover design by Sweet 'n Spicy Designs
ISBN: 978-1-964063-29-4

I care about quality, so if you find something in error, please contact me via email at
shirleen@shirleendavies.com

Description

She's a big city photographer determined to document the West.
He's a no-nonsense rancher focused on growing the family ranch.
Neither intends to back down first.

Molly O'Sullivan is an independent young lady. Determined to follow her own path, she leaves the privileges of her parents' Chicago home to document the West with her photographs and stories. No one will stand in her way, including the much too handsome, obnoxious rancher from the most prominent family in southern Montana.

Elijah Beckett has no plans to change his life. A hard-bitten rancher, Elijah works long days alongside his mother and siblings to keep the ranch growing. In no scenario do his plans include marriage and children... until his life is upended when a vivacious city woman bursts into his life.

To his disappointment, not rustlers or bank robbers, nor being surrounded by a group of Crow Indians, thwarts her plans. Molly is gracious, determined, and annoyingly beautiful, which irritates Elijah even more.

As the town accepts her with open arms, Elijah realizes there is but one course of action left.

Wait her out and celebrate the day she boards the train for anywhere except his small Montana community.

Wild Spirit Revival, Book One in the Montana Becketts ♦ Wild Spirit Ranch historical western romance series, is a clean and wholesome, full-length novel with an HEA and no cliffhanger.

Table of Contents

Chapter One	1
Chapter Two	10
Chapter Three	20
Chapter Four	28
Chapter Five	37
Chapter Six	47
Chapter Seven	57
Chapter Eight	65
Chapter Nine	75
Chapter Ten	84
Chapter Eleven	95
Chapter Twelve	102
Chapter Thirteen	112
Chapter Fourteen	122
Chapter Fifteen	129
Chapter Sixteen	140
Chapter Seventeen	150
Chapter Eighteen	160
Chapter Nineteen	168
Chapter Twenty	178
Chapter Twenty-One	187
Chapter Twenty-Two	196
Chapter Twenty-Three	204

Epilogue	212
A Note from Shirleen	217
Books by Shirleen Davies	219
About Shirleen	225

Wild Spirit Revival

Chapter One

Montana
June 1880

Molly O'Sullivan rubbed her backside for the hundredth time, watching the miles rush by from her spot at the window on the westbound train. Since leaving her home in Chicago, she'd passed through several states and more towns than she could recall. Illinois, Wisconsin, Minnesota, North Dakota, and half of Montana were now behind her.

Though expected, she jumped when the whistle sounded, signaling their approach to Bozeman. Her last stop for now.

The back door to her car opened and closed, a familiar sound after so many miles. The hard object poking behind her ear caused Molly to still. The low, hard voice turned her blood cold.

"Smile as if you know me, and put your money and jewelry into this pouch." The man handed her a suede bag.

She stared at it, unmoving, until he poked her

harder with what Molly believed was the barrel of a gun. Of all the places she could've sat down, why was it at the back of the car, with everyone else facing forward? Unless someone turned around, they'd never learn what was happening a few feet behind them. Reaching into a small silk purse, she extracted a roll of bills.

"This is all I have with me." She slid it into the pouch.

"That thing you've got pinned to your coat. Put it in, too."

"No."

He tapped the barrel against her skull. "No?"

"No," she whispered. "It was my grandmother's. I'll not turn it over to you."

"Fine with me." He reached out and ripped it off her coat.

She gasped, unable to do more before he brushed past her and rushed to the next car. The whistle blew again, shaking her from the stunned surprise, reminding her they were almost to their next stop.

Grabbing her purse, she ran toward the next car, almost falling when the engineer applied the brakes. Steadying herself, Molly moved from one car to the next, looking for the thief. As the train continued to slow, she braced herself.

She knew his face and what he was wearing. Before the train came to a complete stop, Molly jumped down, looking to the front and the back, spotting the miscreant hop off two cars in front of her.

Shouting and pointing for someone to stop the

thief, she charged ahead. Running as fast as possible while wearing a long skirt and men's boots, she could see him jerking around travelers and townsfolk, putting more distance between them.

Gritting her teeth, she continued while shouting once more for help. As she ran past them, people eyed her as if she were the criminal. Spotting him race around a corner, she followed, sure she'd lost him.

Taking the corner, she plowed into an immovable object with a gasp, bounced backward, and landed on her behind. Shaking her head, Molly glared at the man who stood over her.

"Are you all right?" He held out a hand, which she ignored, preferring to stand on her own.

She glanced around, then turned in a circle. "Did you see where he went?"

"Who?"

Eyes afire, she stared at him. "The man who ran around the corner just before me. Which way did he go?"

"Sorry, ma'am. I didn't see a man running. Just you, a second before you almost busted over me."

She scoffed. "You're as hard as a stone building. Are you sure you didn't see anyone?"

He shook his head. "No."

"That's not possible. I was right behind him before he came this way."

"No one came this way."

"Then you're blind as well as daft." She puffed out a breath, her chest heaving.

He raised a brow. "Daft?"

She tapped the side of her head. "Daft. Up here. Anyone with sense would've known something was wrong when he ran this way."

Scratching the back of his neck, he stared at his boots before meeting her hostile gaze with one of his own. "You're sure he came this way?"

Molly set fisted hands on her waist and glared at him. "Are you deaf? I'm positive he ran this way. He stole my money and a watch my grandmother gave me, and I'm not going to let him get away." She turned to leave when he grabbed her arm.

"Tell the sheriff. Let him and his deputies find the thief."

"He'll be long gone by then." She tugged her arm free of his grasp and tried to hurry away before he grabbed her arm again.

"Look, the sheriff here is a good man. If you give him the thief's description, he'll have his men scour the town." When he saw a slow smile form on her face, he relaxed.

Glancing over her shoulder to see one of the deputies, he was about to call out to the man when she once again shrugged off his grasp and took off.

He placed his hands on his hips and shook his head. Even wearing a skirt and boots, she shot away from him, pumping her legs faster than he'd thought possible.

"What's going on?"

Eli Beckett turned to see Deputy Angus McGregor standing beside him, shielding his eyes to look down the street.

"Is that a woman running in the middle of the street?"

Eli nodded. "Sure is."

"Where's she headed?"

"She's after the thief who stole money and a watch from her." He looked at Angus. "They were on the train." Eli tapped his temple. "I don't think the woman's right in the head."

"Then, I'd better go after her. If she's deranged, it'd be best to get her off the street and someplace safe. Maybe the doc can help her."

He nodded. "Good idea. The doc should keep watch on her for a bit. I've got to get the supplies back to the ranch." Eli turned away, then stopped. "She's tricky, as well as daft. Don't let her sweet talk you."

Long strides took him toward Bozeman's general store, his thoughts still on the crazed woman. She was a menace. It would do her good to sit a few hours in the doctor's office and cool off.

The Bozeman railroad station bustled with activity as Molly O'Sullivan maneuvered through the crowd. The cacophony of chattering passengers filled the air, but Molly's emerald eyes remained fixed on the clerk's counter.

Gandy Broom's round face lit up as Molly approached. "What can I do for you, ma'am?"

Her lips quirked into a smile. "I'm Molly O'Sullivan. I was a passenger on the train. I've come to retrieve my equipment and belongings."

"Of course, of course." Gandy glanced to the floor beside him. "I've been keepin' 'em safe and sound for you." Bending down, he hauled the wood box filled with photographic equipment around the counter before retrieving a trunk and a large satchel. "Three items, correct?"

As he set her belongings beside him, her gaze wandered, taking in the station's rustic charm. Though the station was new, the windows were already crusted with dirt, and the scent of coal smoke lingered in the air. She couldn't help but feel a twinge of excitement at the prospect of capturing Bozeman's essence through her lens.

"Yes, just the three. Mr..."

"Broom. Most people call me Gandy."

She smiled, curiosity getting the better of her. "Mr. Broom, I assume you know everyone living around here. What can you tell me about Bozeman?"

His eyes twinkled. "Oh, Bozeman's a right fine place, miss. Full of opportunity for those willin' to seize it. Why, just last week, we had a lady open up a millinery shop on Main Street. Caused quite a stir, I tell you."

Her eyebrows rose with interest. "A woman-owned business? That's wonderful."

"Oh, we've got our fair share of forward-thinkin' folks here." He chuckled. "Bozeman's growin' fast, and with that comes new ideas."

She studied her belongings, bending to run a hand over her camera case. "Thank you for holding these for me, Mr. Broom."

Gandy beamed. "Happy to help, Miss O'Sullivan. Now, I reckon you'll be needin' a place to stay. The Bozeman Hotel down the street is mighty fine, and they've probably got rooms available."

"That would be perfect. I'm afraid I'll need some assistance with my belongings."

Gandy turned to wave at a young boy sweeping nearby. "Hey, Tommy. Come give Miss O'Sullivan a hand with her things, would you?"

The freckle-faced boy, no more than twelve, bounded over. "Yes, sir, Mr. Broom."

"I'll carry the wood box, Tommy," she said.

"Yes, ma'am." As Tommy began gathering her bags, Molly felt a mix of anticipation and trepidation. She could sense this was the start of her grand adventure in Montana.

"Miss O'Sullivan?" Gandy's voice broke through her reverie. "Is there anything else you need before you head to the hotel?"

She shook her head, a determined glint in her eye. "No, thank you. I believe I'm ready."

As she followed Tommy out of the station, her mind whirled with possibilities. Little did she know her journey in Bozeman was about to take an unexpected turn, one that would challenge her resolve and change her life forever.

Molly sank onto the bed in her hotel room, her fingers absently tracing the intricate floral pattern on the quilt. The afternoon sun filtered through the lace curtains, reminding her of what she had planned for the rest of the day. She sighed, her mind drifting back to the unpleasant encounter with the boorish man at the train station.

"Of all the nerve," she muttered. "I hope I never have to lay eyes on the insufferable brute again."

Molly's teeth worried her lower lip as she replayed the scene in her mind. The man's arrogant smirk, his dismissive tone. It made her blood boil. She shook her head, determined not to let one sour interaction taint her entire experience in Bozeman.

"Come now, Molly," she chided herself. "You didn't come all this way to dwell on one unpleasant man."

She checked herself in the mirror, adjusting her hat and smoothing her dress. Ready to explore and photograph, she first had to meet Deputy McGregor at the sheriff's office.

With renewed vigor, she gathered her camera equipment. Stepping out onto the bustling streets of Bozeman, her spirits lifted. The town hummed with activity. Shopkeepers arranged displays, children chased each other down the sidewalk, and the distant clang of a blacksmith's hammer drew her attention. As did the sign declaring the building held the jail.

Stepping inside, she set down her camera case beside a scarred desk. The man sitting behind it looked and stood.

"Ma'am. What can I do for you?"

"Are you a deputy?"

"Sheriff Jud Foster."

"Pleased to meet you. I'm Molly O'Sullivan, and I've come to report a theft."

"Ah. Deputy McGregor said you'd be coming by. Sit down and tell me the details."

She eyed the man, certain he was much too young to hold the position of sheriff. Nevertheless, Molly took a seat and explained everything, from the moment the gun pressed against her head to losing him in the streets of Bozeman.

"When may I get my belongings back, Sheriff?"

Jud studied her a moment. "First, we have to find the thief. With luck, he still has the money and watch with him."

"You don't believe he will?"

"He might. Then again, he may have already pawned the watch and left town."

Shoulders slumping, she lifted her chin. "Then I should leave and let you start searching for him." Standing, she faced Jud. "I'm staying at the Bozeman Hotel. Please get word to me right away once he's in custody."

Lifting her camera case, she walked outside, not hearing the sheriff's soft chuckle.

Chapter Two

Her next stop was a quaint general store, its windows filled with an eclectic array of goods. A bell chimed as she entered. A portly man with a jovial smile greeted her.

"Welcome. I'm Esau Perkins. What can I do for you today?" His gaze landed on the wooden box she set on the floor.

"Hello, Mr. Perkins. I'm Molly O'Sullivan, a photographer new to town. I was hoping to capture some images of Bozeman's businesses and perhaps learn a bit about the area."

"A photographer, you say? We haven't had one for a while. Not sense, well…best not to dwell on what happened to him. You're more than welcome to take pictures of my store, Miss O'Sullivan."

As Molly set up her camera, curiosity settled over her. "What happened to the last photographer, if you don't mind my asking?"

Esau's expression darkened. "Oh, it's a bit of a sore subject around here. Poor fella met an untimely end while trying to photograph some unsavory characters passing through town. But don't you worry your pretty head about his fate. Bozeman's a fine place, full of good folks."

"I see. Well, Mr. Perkins, perhaps you could tell me about some of the other businesses in town while I work?"

As she captured images of the store's interior, Esau regaled her with tales of Bozeman's colorful inhabitants and thriving community. With each image, Molly felt a growing excitement for the anticipated adventures ahead.

The following morning, Molly set out early, her camera box slung over her shoulder and a newfound determination in her step. The streets of Bozeman were already bustling with activity, the air filled with the scent of freshly baked bread and the sound of horses' hooves on packed dirt.

As she rounded a corner, Molly nearly collided with a tall, striking woman in a crisp white apron. "Oh, I do beg your pardon."

The woman's face broke into a grin when she noticed the wooden box. "No harm done, dear. You must be the photographer everyone's been talking about."

Molly nodded, extending her hand. "Molly O'Sullivan, at your service."

"Clara Hawkins," the woman replied, shaking Molly's hand firmly. "I own the Bozeman Bakery just down the street. You simply must come by and take some photographs. I'd love to show off my girls hard at work."

Molly's eyes widened. "Your girls?"

Clara chuckled. "The bakery opened five years ago, and I've only hired women. If they don't know how to bake, they learn and become very loyal. It also keeps them away from less savory work." She shot Molly a knowing look. "Bozeman's got quite a few women who own businesses around here."

Intrigued, she followed Clara to the bakery, curious as to the woman's history. "Have you always lived in Bozeman, Mrs. Hawkins?"

"Came out here with my husband about ten years ago. When he passed, I knew I had to make my own way. Turns out, I had quite the knack for baking."

Entering the bakery, the sweet aroma of cinnamon and sugar enveloped them. Three young women bustled about, kneading dough and arranging pastries.

"Ladies," Clara called out. "This is Miss O'Sullivan. She's going to take some photographs of us at work."

While Molly set up her equipment, she engaged the women in conversation, marveling at their stories of independence and determination. As she captured image after image, she found herself deeply moved by the strength and resilience of these frontier women.

"If you're interested, a group of women who own

businesses are meeting tomorrow morning. It's in the dining room of the Bozeman Hotel."

"Oh, that's where I'm staying. I'd love to attend if it wouldn't be an intrusion."

"No intrusion at all. Would you mind taking a few minutes to share how you became a photographer?" Clara asked.

"Not at all. It isn't a complicated story, so it won't take much time."

Clara tapped a finger against her lips. "You know, if you're looking for more to photograph, you might want to head down to Mystic. It's a small town south of here. They have some colorful characters and beautiful scenery."

Molly's interest was piqued. "Mystic? I hadn't heard of it. How far is it?"

"Oh, not far at all. About eleven miles south. You can take the stagecoach."

Leaving the bakery a short time later, Molly considered her options. Mystic could be the kind of place she'd come west to document. First, she had more of Bozeman to explore, more stories to uncover, and more remarkable women to meet. And hopefully, a thief arrested and brought to justice.

Molly hurried to dress the following morning, her heart beating with anticipation. She smoothed her simple cotton dress and adjusted the cameo pinned to the bodice, eager to make a good impression at the breakfast meeting.

Leaving her room, she rushed down the stairs, her gaze sparkling with excitement. Entering the hotel's dining room, a tall, striking woman, with dark hair pinned neatly back, approached her with an outstretched hand.

"You must be Molly," she said, her voice measured and confident. "I'm Mrs. Ada Green. Welcome to our little gathering."

Molly shook her hand enthusiastically. "It's a pleasure to meet you, Mrs. Green."

As Ada led her to the table, Molly's gaze swept across the room, taking in the diverse group of women seated around it. Her heart swelled with a sense of belonging she hadn't felt since leaving Chicago.

"Ladies," Ada announced, "this is Molly O'Sullivan, the photographer Clara told us about."

A chorus of greetings followed, and Molly found herself seated between a graceful blonde woman and a stern-looking older lady with steel-gray hair.

The blonde turned to her with a smile. "I'm Evelyn Graham, the schoolteacher in Mystic. It's wonderful to meet you, Molly."

Molly's eyes widened. "Mystic? I've just heard about it yesterday. It sounds fascinating."

"Oh, it is. You must visit. The landscapes alone are worth the trip."

"You made the long trip for this meeting?" Molly asked.

Evelyn chuckled. "Oh, no. School isn't in session right now, so I took the stage to Bozeman with my mother. We'll spend a few days before returning to Mystic."

As plates of eggs and bacon were served, the conversation flowed from one topic to another. Molly listened, offering her own thoughts and experiences when she thought it appropriate.

"The biggest challenge is getting men to take our businesses seriously," a woman named Agnes said. "They seem to think we'll swoon at the first sign of trouble or controversy. If a woman is married, the bank will require a loan be in her husband's name. It's humiliating."

Ada nodded. "That's precisely why we established our own fund for women."

Molly's eyes widened. "You have a fund just for women?"

"Oh, yes," Ada answered. "We loan money the same as banks. The women must make monthly payments."

"Our interest rate is a little lower than the bank's," Clara said with a mischievous grin.

"Where does the money come from?" Molly asked.

Ada looked around the room. "From this group, as well as a few other women who don't want their names connected to us. It's why gatherings such as ours are so important. We need to support each other and share information."

"Mother and I support this group," Evelyn said. "Father doesn't know we're involved. As the president of the Bank of Mystic, he'd be quite agitated at what these women are doing for each other."

As the meal progressed, Molly felt a growing sense of camaraderie with these remarkable women. Their stories of perseverance and triumph in the face of adversity stirred something deep within her.

"What about you, Molly?" Evelyn asked. "What brought you out west?"

She hesitated, her thoughts drifting to the evening she told her parents of her decision to leave Chicago. "I suppose I was looking for adventure. A chance to see the country and capture it through my lens."

The stern-looking woman beside her harrumphed. "Adventure, is it? Well, you'll find plenty of that out here, missy. Just be careful it doesn't swallow you whole."

Molly turned to her, intrigued. "What do you mean?"

The woman's eyes glinted. "This part of the country can be unforgiving, especially to those who aren't prepared for its challenges. You seem like a smart girl, but don't let your eagerness blind you to the dangers."

A hush fell over the table, and Molly felt a shiver run down her spine. The woman's words hung in the air, a stark reminder of the untamed nature of the frontier. As she opened her mouth to respond, a commotion outside the hotel caught everyone's attention. The sound of pounding hooves and shouting voices filled the air, and the women rushed to the window to see what was happening.

As the women peered out the window, Molly's curiosity got the better of her. She leaned forward, wishing she had her camera set up to catch the action outside.

"My word," exclaimed Mrs. Agnes Abernathy, a plump woman with kind eyes. "It looks like trouble's coming. It's nine in the morning. Surely, those men don't plan to enter the saloon."

Outside, a group of rough-looking men on horseback had pulled up in front of the saloon across the street. Their loud voices and boisterous laughter carried through the air, setting Molly's nerves on edge.

Agnes turned to Molly, her expression serious. "Speaking of dangers, dear, I hope you're not planning on opening a portraiture store here in Bozeman."

Molly blinked, surprised by the sudden change in topic. "I hadn't given it much thought. Why do you ask?"

The older woman's face clouded with concern. "Well, we had a photographer here not too long ago. Poor fellow met a rather... unfortunate end."

Molly leaned in. "I heard he died."

Agnes lowered her voice, glancing at the commotion outside. "He was taking a photograph of a group of gunslingers passing through town. One moment, he was adjusting his camera. The next..." She trailed off, shaking her head.

Molly felt a chill run down her spine. "You mean he was...?"

"Shot dead, right there in the street," Agnes finished, her expression grim. "Someone, no one knows who, didn't want him taking pictures of the gunslingers, I'm afraid."

Molly's earlier excitement faded at this sobering tale. She thought of her own camera, safely tucked away in its case. "That's terrible," she murmured.

Clara spoke up. "So, Molly, what are your plans then? Surely, you're not thinking of setting up shop here after hearing what happened."

Molly took a deep breath, gathering her thoughts. "Actually, I have something else in mind. I'm planning to photograph the area between Bozeman and the Wyoming border before traveling into Yellowstone for the rest of the summer. From there, I hope to travel to Seattle."

The women exchanged glances, a mix of curiosity and concern on their faces.

"Quite an undertaking," Clara remarked.

"The landscapes, the people, the spirit of the West—I want to capture it all."

Agnes raised an eyebrow. "Yellowstone? My dear, that's no place for a young woman alone."

Molly straightened her shoulders, a determined set to her jaw. "I may be young, but I'm capable." She thought about trekking through the national park and wondered if her capabilities were enough.

As the women around her murmured their thoughts on her ambitious plans, Molly's attention was drawn back to the window. The rowdy group outside had dismounted, and one man in particular caught her eye. He was tall, with a shock of white hair and a dangerous glint in his eye visible even from this distance.

When the man whirled around, his gaze appeared to lock on Molly. A chill ran through her at the stark look in his eyes. Backing away from the window, she swallowed the fear his gaze prompted, praying to never come face to face with the terrifying gunman.

Chapter Three

Molly stepped out of Mrs. Henderson's millinery shop, pleased with the pictures she'd taken of the woman and her displays. Taking a step away, she turned at the woman's voice.

Mrs. Henderson stood in the shop's doorway. "Oh, Miss O'Sullivan, I can't thank you enough. To think, my little shop will be immortalized in your photographs."

"It's my pleasure. Your hats are true works of art, and the country should know about the talented women of Bozeman."

Continuing along the boardwalk, Molly thought about Mrs. Henderson's comment about her shop being immortalized. It was a concept she didn't often consider. Each image was a testament to the strength and determination of these frontier women.

Molly headed toward the hotel, recalling her conversation with Ada Green when the morning meeting adjourned. Molly had mentioned the need to find a place to develop her photographs. To her shock, Ada owned the building where the previous photographer had his shop. It was still available with the dark room intact, including chemicals.

Ada had been gracious enough to show Molly the shop. To her delight, it was indeed in good shape, with shelves of chemicals and a dark-box for her dry-plate photography. She offered to purchase the use of the dark room and chemicals, but Ada had waved her off, saying Molly could use whatever she wanted. It was an unexpected gift.

As she made her way down the bustling street, Molly's thoughts drifted to her impending departure. A mixture of excitement and apprehension swirled in her chest. The town of Mystic was an unknown, full of potential dangers and opportunities alike.

Arriving at Abernathy's Apothecary, Molly was greeted by the tinkling of a bell above the door. The scent of herbs and tinctures filled the air as she stepped inside.

"Miss O'Sullivan," Agnes Abernathy called from behind the counter. "Right on time. Shall we begin?"

As Molly set up her equipment, she engaged Agnes in conversation. "Your shop is fascinating. How did you come to open an apothecary in Bozeman?"

Agnes's eyes lit up as she recounted arriving in the frontier town with her now deceased husband. They'd opened the apothecary, working side by side for years until his passing. Agnes continued the shop alone, offering the same medicines as when her husband had been alive.

Molly found herself captivated by the woman's

tale of perseverance and ingenuity. With each click of the camera shutter, Molly felt she was capturing not just an image but a piece of Bozeman's living history.

After bidding farewell to Agnes, she made her way to the stagecoach office. The gruff ticket agent, Mr. Hawkins, eyed her warily as she approached the counter.

"One ticket to Mystic for tomorrow's coach, please," she requested, her voice steady despite the butterflies in her stomach.

"Mystic, eh? Not many ladies travel there alone. You sure about this, miss?"

Her jaw tightened. "Quite sure, thank you."

As she exited the office, ticket in hand, Molly couldn't shake the feeling her adventure was about to take an unexpected turn. Little did she know, the real challenges were yet to come.

The stagecoach creaked and swayed as Molly settled into her seat, her camera equipment safely stowed beneath. She found herself wedged between the window and a rotund drummer, his leather satchel clutched tightly to his chest. Across from them sat a couple with a young daughter, the child's excited chatter filling the cramped space.

"Mama, look! Horses!" The little girl bounced on the seat.

Her mother smiled. "Yes, dear. Now, please sit

still. It won't be long until we reach Mystic."

Molly's gaze drifted out the window as the coach lurched forward, the rhythmic clop of hooves accompanying their departure from Bozeman. The landscape unfurled before her like a living canvas. Rolling hills gave way to rugged mountains, their peaks shrouded in mist.

"First time to Mystic, miss?" the drummer inquired, his voice jolting Molly from her reverie.

She offered a polite smile. "Yes, it is. I'm a photographer, documenting the frontier."

The man's eyebrows shot up. "A lady photographer. I've always wanted to try one of those contraptions. My name's Gus Thornton, traveling salesman extraordinaire," he said with a wink.

As Gus launched into a tale about his travels selling various wares, Molly's thoughts drifted back to her encounter with the obnoxious man in Bozeman. His arrogant smirk and dismissive tone still made her blood boil.

"You all right there, miss?" Gus asked, noticing her furrowed brow. "Looks like you've bitten into a sour apple."

Molly forced a laugh. "Just remembering an unpleasant encounter."

The little girl across from them piped up, "Did a mean person make you sad? Mama says when people are mean, it's 'cause they're sad themselves."

Molly's expression softened. "Your mama sounds very wise. What's your name, sweetheart?"

"I'm Mary! We're going to visit my grandpa in

Mystic. Do you have a grandpa there, too?"

As Molly engaged in conversation with Mary and her parents, the stagecoach continued its journey. The passing scenery captivated her, each bend in the road revealing new wonders.

Suddenly, the coach jerked to a halt, nearly throwing Molly from her seat. The driver's urgent and fearful shout reached them.

"Ladies and gentlemen! We've got a problem up ahead."

The passengers exchanged worried glances as the driver's words hung in the air. Molly's heart raced as she peered out the window, straining to see what had caused their sudden stop.

"What kind of problem?" the drummer beside her called out, his voice tinged with anxiety.

The driver's response was cut short by the sound of hoofbeats approaching. Molly's breath caught in her throat as she saw three riders emerging from the dust, their faces obscured by bandanas.

"Everybody out!" a gruff voice commanded. "Nice and slow, hands where we can see 'em."

Mary whimpered, clinging to her mother. Molly's fingers traced the watch pinned to her dress. Sheriff Foster had returned it to her the night before while she ate supper at the hotel.

Ezra Gibbons, the owner of Bozeman's livery and stables, had found it on the ground inside one of the stalls. Gibbons had given a description of the man whose horse had been in the stall. It matched with what Molly had provided the sheriff. She was not going to give it up a second time. Quickly, she removed the watch, bent, and slid it into her boot.

As they filed out of the coach, Molly's eyes darted around, assessing the situation. The lead bandit, a tall man with piercing eyes, dismounted and approached the group.

"All right, folks. No one will get hurt if you do exactly what I say. Place your valuables in this bag, and don't do anything foolish."

Molly's jaw clenched. She couldn't lose her camera equipment. As the hat made its way down the line, she searched for a way out.

Everyone turned when a commotion erupted from the front of the coach. The driver had managed to pull a hidden revolver, aiming it at the bandits.

"Drop your weapons!" he shouted, his voice steadier now. Beside him, the guard pointed his rifle toward the outlaws. Undeterred, the bandits began firing.

As shots rang out, Molly and the other passengers scrambled for cover. Her heart pounded as they crouched behind a large boulder, the sounds of the skirmish echoing around them.

"What do we do now?" Mary's father asked, his voice laced with fear.

Molly peered around the rock, seeing one outlaw on the ground and the stagecoach driver slumped in his seat. "We need to get help..."

She trailed off as she spotted something in the distance. A cloud of dust moving rapidly toward them. Help, or more trouble?

As the riders drew closer, Molly's eyes widened. If she weren't mistaken, leading the group was a familiar face. The very man she'd hoped to avoid.

The stranger from Bozeman thundered toward them, leading a group of riders. As they approached, Molly could make out his features. He had the same rugged jawline and piercing eyes as the man at the train station.

"Stay down!" His voice carried over the chaos.

Molly watched, torn between relief and frustration, as the newcomers engaged the bandits. The air filled with gunshots and shouts, dust swirling around the scene.

The man from Bozeman may become her unlikely savior.

"Who is that man?" Mary's mother whispered, clutching her daughter close.

Molly shook her head, her eyes never leaving the action. "Someone I'd hoped never to see again," she muttered.

The skirmish was intense but brief. Within minutes, the outlaws were subdued, their weapons tossed aside as they raised their hands in surrender.

When the dust settled, the stranger dismounted and strode toward their hiding spot. Molly steeled herself, stepping out from behind the boulder.

"Figure the odds," he drawled, a smirk playing at the corners of his mouth. "Seems like trouble follows you, Miss...?"

"Molly," she replied curtly. "Molly O'Sullivan. And I had everything under control."

He raised an eyebrow, his gaze sweeping over the stagecoach guard and the shaken passengers. "Clearly."

Before she could retort, Mary tugged at her skirt. "Miss Molly, are we safe now?"

Molly softened, kneeling down to the child's level. "Yes, Mary. We're safe now."

The stranger's expression changed, a flicker of something crossing his face. He held out his hand to a short, portly male passenger.

"Name's Elijah Beckett."

"Gus Thornton." He mopped his forehead with a handkerchief before stuffing it into a pocket.

"I'm Michael Crane," Mary's father said, shaking Elijah's hand. "This is my wife, Marla, and daughter, Mary. I don't know how to thank you, Mr. Beckett. You saved all of us."

"No thanks necessary." Elijah looked back at the stage. "It appears you folks could use a ride into town. One of us will sit up top and drive the stage. Let's get you back in the coach."

As the passengers gathered their scattered belongings, Molly found herself stealing glances at Elijah. There was something about him. To her disgust, she found herself both intrigued and annoyed.

Chapter Four

The stagecoach rumbled to a halt in front of Mystic's stagecoach station, its wooden wheels creaking in protest. Molly O'Sullivan exhaled, her shoulders sagging with relief as she peered out at the town. The harrowing journey, marred by the attempted robbery, had left her both exhilarated and exhausted.

"We made it," she murmured, more to herself than to her fellow passengers.

Gus Thornton, seated next to her, chuckled. "Yes, we did. We have those Beckett boys to thank for arriving alive."

Molly's eyes narrowed at the mention of the Becketts. Elijah's manner during their second encounter grated on her.

"I suppose," she replied curtly, glancing outside.

The guard was already walking toward the doctor's office with the wounded driver in his arms.

As the stage office clerk opened the coach door, Molly caught sight of three tall figures escorting a group of bound men down the street. The Beckett brothers, she realized, were leading the outlaws to jail.

Elijah Beckett's commanding presence was unmistakable as they marched the outlaws forward. His younger brothers, Joshua and Nathan, flanked the group, their movements coordinated and efficient.

"Move along," Elijah barked at one of the prisoners who'd slowed his pace. "You've caused enough trouble for one day."

Joshua, ever the peacemaker, placed a calming hand on his brother's shoulder. "Easy, Elijah. They're not going anywhere now."

As Molly stepped down from the coach, her gaze locked with Elijah's for a brief moment before he looked away.

She found herself torn between gratitude for their rescue and irritation at Elijah's brusque manner. Though she couldn't deny the competence with which the brothers handled the situation, there was something about Elijah she couldn't quite describe. Whatever it was, she found her mind going back to him more often than she liked.

"Miss O'Sullivan," Gus called out, nodding at her belongings on the boardwalk. "I believe these are yours. I didn't want to leave them unattended."

Grateful for the distraction, Molly turned to the drummer. "Thank you, Gus."

"Do you need help getting them to the hotel?"

"I can do it, ma'am." A boy of about fourteen rushed forward. "I'm Eddie, and I'll carry as much as you want me to."

Smiling, Molly extended her hand. "I'm Miss O'Sullivan, Eddie, and I'd appreciate your help."

Sheriff Brodie Gaines stood in the doorway of the jailhouse, his broad shoulders filling the frame as he watched the Beckett brothers approaching with their captives. His eyes narrowed, a mixture of surprise and approval crossing his face.

"Well, I'll be," he muttered, turning to his deputy. "Jubal, appears we've got some unexpected guests."

Deputy Jubal Whitton appeared at his side, his lanky frame a contrast to the sheriff's solid build. "Beckett boys bringing in trouble again?" A hint of amusement could be heard in his voice.

As Elijah, Joshua, and Nathan marched the outlaws toward the jail, the sheriff stepped forward, his hand resting on his holster. "Afternoon, boys. Seems you've had an eventful day."

Elijah nodded. "Caught these men trying to rob the stagecoach. Thought you might want to have a word with them."

The sheriff raised a brow. "Well, let's get them situated inside." He turned toward his deputy. "Jube, grab the keys."

Once the outlaws were securely locked away, the Beckett brothers gathered outside the jailhouse. Elijah turned to his siblings.

"I could use a drink before we ride back to the

ranch."

Joshua nodded, a smile playing on his lips. "Buffalo Run?"

"You read my mind, Josh." Nathan grinned, already heading toward the tavern.

As they walked, the tension from earlier began to dissipate. Nathan, unable to contain his enthusiasm, recounted the events to his brothers. "Did you see the look on the big fella's face when Elijah got the drop on him?"

Joshua chuckled. "You did good out there, Nate. Kept your head when it counted."

"You both did," Elijah said. "Proud to ride with you."

The warmth of his rare praise hung in the air as they pushed through the doors of Buffalo Run Tavern. The familiar smell of tobacco enveloped them, a welcome respite from the day's excitement. Although it was a tavern, Buffalo Run served some of the best food in Mystic, and boasted a clientele of both men and women.

As they settled at a table, Joshua couldn't help but notice Elijah's gaze roaming the room, as if searching for someone. "Hoping to see that feisty redhead from the stagecoach?"

Elijah's jaw tightened as he gave a slight shake of his head. "Making sure no one followed us in here. I'm not convinced we brought in all the outlaws responsible for stopping the stagecoach."

"You mean, there may have been a lookout?" Joshua asked.

Elijah gave a slow nod as the bartender brought over three beers.

Nathan raised his beer. "To the safe return of the passengers to Mystic."

As they clinked their glasses together, Elijah couldn't shake the image of the determined woman from the stagecoach. Taking another sip of his beer, his gaze moved to the entrance.

The swinging doors creaked open, drawing the attention of the patrons. Molly O'Sullivan strode in, her chin held high despite the curious stares from the male crowd. Her gaze swept the room, briefly locking with Elijah's before she chose a table far from the Beckett brothers.

As she settled into her seat, she couldn't help feeling a thrill of defiance. She'd come to Montana to forge her own path, and she wasn't about to let societal expectations hold her back. The tavern, with its rough-hewn wooden tables and smoky atmosphere, was a far cry from the tea rooms of Boston. Molly found she rather liked it.

A barmaid approached, eyebrows raised in surprise. "What can I get for you, miss?"

Molly smiled, her voice clear and confident. "A sarsaparilla, please. What do you have to eat?"

"Today's special is beef stew."

"I'll also have a bowl of the stew."

As the barmaid walked away, Molly felt a presence looming over her. She looked up to find Elijah Beckett standing at her table, his eyes narrowed in a mixture of curiosity and disapproval.

"Well, Miss O'Sullivan," he drawled, his voice low and gravelly. "I must say, I'm surprised to see a lady such as yourself in a place like this."

Molly didn't flinch as she met his gaze. "And why is that, Mr. Beckett? Surely, a woman is as capable of enjoying a meal in a tavern as any man."

Elijah lifted a brow. "It's not about capability, miss. It's about propriety. This isn't exactly a place for—"

"For what?" Molly interrupted, her voice sharp. "For independent women who make their own choices? I assure you, Mr. Beckett, I'm quite capable of handling myself in any establishment, tavern or otherwise."

A muscle twitched in Elijah's jaw. "I didn't mean to offend," he said, though his tone suggested otherwise. "I'm merely concerned for your safety and reputation."

She leaned back in her chair, a smile playing on her lips. "Your concern is noted but unnecessary. Now, if you'll excuse me, I believe my sarsaparilla is arriving."

As the barmaid set down her drink, Molly turned her attention away from Elijah, dismissing him. She could feel his gaze on her for several more seconds before she heard him walk away.

Molly refused to be intimidated by anyone. She'd come to Mystic on a mission to photograph the wonders of the frontier. She wasn't about to let anyone, not even the ruggedly handsome Elijah Beckett, make her feel out of place. Molly tensed when she sensed his return. She glanced up to find him once again by her side.

Elijah's eyes narrowed, a flash of annoyance crossing his face. "Suit yourself, Miss O'Sullivan. Just don't come crying for help when you find yourself in over your head."

With a curt nod, Elijah turned on his heel and strode back to where his brothers sat, his boots echoing on the worn wooden floor. As he approached their table, Joshua raised an eyebrow, a smirk playing at the corners of his mouth.

"Well," Joshua drawled, "that was quite the display of charm. I'm surprised she didn't swoon right into your arms."

Nathan chuckled, taking a swig of his beer. "Yeah, Eli. You've got all the subtlety of a bull in a China shop when it comes to women."

Elijah scowled, dropping heavily into his chair. "I wasn't trying to charm her," he growled. "The woman's more stubborn than a mule. Can't she see it's not proper for her to be here?"

Joshua leaned in, his voice lowered. "And since when did you become the arbiter of propriety, big brother? I seem to recall a certain incident with Widow Johnson's daughter a while back."

"That was different. A complete misunderstanding," Elijah muttered, a hint of color rising to his cheeks. He glanced over his shoulder at Molly, who was pointedly ignoring them as she sipped her sarsaparilla. "She's... infuriating."

Nathan grinned, clasping Elijah on the shoulder.

"Sounds to me as if you're more interested than you'd care to admit. Never seen a woman get under your skin the way this one has."

Elijah shrugged off his brother's hand. "Don't be ridiculous. I'm just concerned about the reputation of our town. What if every woman started frequenting taverns?"

"Then maybe we'd have some better company than your sour face," Joshua quipped, earning a laugh from Nathan and a glare from Elijah.

As the brothers continued their playful banter, Elijah couldn't help stealing another glance at Molly. There was something about her defiance, her unwillingness to back down. Her attitude irritated and intrigued him. He shook his head, trying to clear his thoughts. She was trouble, plain and simple. And the last thing Elijah Beckett needed was trouble in his life.

Lifting his glass to his lips, he took a long swig, trying to focus on his brothers' conversation. Unfortunately, his gaze kept drifting back to Molly, drawn like a magnet to her fiery hair and determined posture.

"Elijah?" Joshua snapped his fingers in front of his brother's face. "You still with us?"

He started, nearly spilling his beer. "What?"

Nathan leaned in, a mischievous glint in his eye. "You sure? Because it seems you're more interested in our new arrival than in discussing ranch business."

"I'm just... keeping an eye on her," Elijah muttered, his jaw clenching. "Someone's got to make sure she doesn't cause any trouble."

Joshua rolled his eyes. "Right. Because a woman eating stew is such a threat to our way of life."

Elijah scowled, drained the last of his beer, and stood. "We should head back to the ranch. Those chores won't take care of themselves."

They made their way to the tavern's exit, Elijah lagging behind. As they reached the door, he couldn't resist one last glance at Molly. To his surprise, he found her looking right back at him, her gaze challenging and curious.

For a moment, their gazes locked, and Elijah felt a jolt of... something. Displeasure? Interest? He couldn't quite name it. He turned away, following his brothers out onto the boardwalk.

As the tavern door swung shut behind them, Molly sat alone at her table, her thoughts swirling. She'd come to Montana seeking adventure and independence. Not once had she expected to encounter a man as interesting as Elijah Beckett. His gruff exterior and apparent disdain for her presence should have been off-putting. Instead, there was something in those stolen glances, as if there was more to him than she anticipated.

"Ridiculous," she muttered to herself, shaking her head. "He's just another narrow-minded man who can't handle a woman thinking for herself."

As she finished her meal and prepared to leave, Molly couldn't shake the feeling her interactions with Elijah Beckett were far from over.

Chapter Five

The sun-drenched, rolling plains of Montana stretched before Molly as she guided her rented buggy toward Wild Spirit Ranch. Her camera equipment bounced on the seat with each jolt of the wheels, a constant reminder of her purpose.

The past two days in Mystic had yielded some promising shots. She could almost hear Casper Jennings' gravelly voice urging her to head south.

"If it's real Montana you're after, Miss O'Sullivan, you'll find it at the Beckett place."

As the sprawling ranch came into view, Molly's heart quickened. The sheer vastness of it took her breath away. According to Casper, owner of Jennings Mercantile & Dry Goods, Wild Spirit Ranch was 150,000 acres of untamed beauty. She pulled up to the main house, a sprawling structure rising from the landscape.

A woman with chestnut hair and striking blue eyes emerged onto the porch, one hand resting on her swollen belly. "Can I help you?" Her voice carried a slight Southern drawl.

Molly climbed down from the buggy. "Good afternoon, ma'am. I'm Molly O'Sullivan. I was hoping to take some photographs of your beautiful ranch. If you have no objection."

The woman's face lit up with a smile. "Oh, how delightful! I'm Jolene Beckett. Please, come in out of this heat."

As Molly followed Jolene inside, she explained her project. "I'm capturing the essence of Montana. Its people and places. Your ranch is spectacular."

Jolene beamed with pride. "We certainly think so. My husband, Grayson, and his brothers have poured their hearts into this land. My mother-in-law, Naomi Beckett, still lives here. She's a widow and a force unto herself. Right now, she's in San Francisco visiting relatives." She paused, studying Molly. "You're welcome to photograph around the house and outbuildings. I'd love to see Montana, and the ranch, through your eyes."

Molly felt a rush of gratitude. "Thank you, Mrs. Beckett. Your kindness means more than you know."

"Please, call me Jolene. Would you care for tea or coffee?"

"Thank you. I'm good, for now."

"Then let me show you around."

Over the next hour, Jolene and Molly walked around the extensive ranch area. Two small barns, one larger one, separate stables, numerous corrals, paddocks, and various sheds for tools underscored the longevity of the ranch.

"I hope you've seen some locations of interest," Jolene said when they returned to the house.

"At least two dozen spots. I won't be able to get it all done before leaving for town."

"Then you'll have to return tomorrow." Jolene smiled.

Molly lost herself in her work, crouching low to capture the weathered grain of the barn door, the play of light across the corral, and several horses grazing in a corral. She was so engrossed in her work, she didn't hear the approaching horses until a familiar voice boomed across the yard.

"What in tarnation is going on here?"

Molly whirled to see Elijah Beckett dismounting, his face a storm cloud of anger. Behind him, a man she assumed was Grayson looked on with confusion.

Elijah strode toward her, eyes blazing. "You! What do you think you're doing on our property?"

Molly stood her ground, chin raised in defiance. "I'm working, Mr. Beckett. Something I believe you're familiar with."

"This isn't some attraction for greenhorns," Elijah growled. "You can't just—"

"Elijah!" Jolene's voice cut through the tension. She waddled toward them, one hand on her back. "I gave Miss O'Sullivan permission to photograph the ranch. She's documenting Montana for a project."

Elijah's jaw clenched, his gaze darting between Molly and his sister-in-law. The muscles in his neck corded as he struggled to rein in his temper.

Molly watched the silent exchange, her own anger

giving way to fascination. There was something in the way Elijah's eyes softened when he looked at Jolene, a protectiveness contradicting his gruff exterior.

Grayson stepped forward, breaking the tense silence. "Well, if Jolene's given her blessing, I don't see the harm." He extended a hand to Molly. "Grayson Beckett. Welcome to Wild Spirit Ranch, Miss O'Sullivan."

As Molly shook his hand, she couldn't help noticing Elijah's deep scowl. She met his gaze, a challenge in her eyes. "I assure you, Mr. Beckett, I mean no disrespect to your home. I'm simply here to capture its beauty."

Elijah's nostrils flared. He opened his mouth to retort, but Jolene placed a gentle hand on his arm. "Why don't you show Miss O'Sullivan around, Elijah? I'm sure she'd appreciate a guide who knows every inch of this land."

Molly's eyes widened. Spend more time with this bristling bear of a man? The very thought sent a shiver down her spine. Though whether from fear or something else, she couldn't quite say.

Molly squared her shoulders, determined not to let Elijah intimidate her. "That won't be necessary, Jolene. I've taken enough photographs for today." She began packing her equipment with swift, practiced movements.

Elijah's narrowed gaze watched her, refraining from any more comments.

As Molly secured her camera in its case, she shot occasional glances at Elijah. His interaction with

Jolene had revealed a side of him she hadn't expected. Protective and gentle. It was a stark contrast to the brusque man who'd confronted her moments ago.

"I do appreciate your hospitality." Molly addressed Jolene and Grayson. "Your ranch is truly spectacular."

Jolene beamed, her hand resting on her swollen belly. "You're welcome back anytime, Miss O'Sullivan. Perhaps next time, you can join us for supper?"

Elijah's head snapped up, his jaw taut. Molly caught the look and felt a flutter in her stomach. Why did his disapproval bother her?

"That's very kind of you," Molly replied, hoisting her equipment into the buggy.

Settling onto the seat, she urged the horse forward. The drive back to Mystic gave her ample time to ponder the mystery of Elijah Beckett. She'd come to Wild Spirit Ranch expecting to capture images of the largest ranch in this part of the frontier. Instead, she found herself grappling with a man who challenged her at every turn.

The buggy rattled along the road back to Mystic, each jolt mirroring the tumult in her thoughts. It was beautiful, but Molly barely noticed, her mind fixated on the perplexing Elijah Beckett.

"Insufferable man," she muttered, gripping the reins tighter.

She huffed, blowing a stray curl from her face. The image of Elijah's gentle interaction with Jolene kept replaying in her mind, at odds with his earlier gruffness.

As Mystic came into view, Molly slowed the buggy. The town was alive with the bustle of early evening. Shopkeepers closed up, ranch hands headed into Buffalo Run Tavern, and children played games before supper. A typical early evening in most towns.

"Miss O'Sullivan," Casper Jennings called from the porch of his mercantile. "How'd the photographing go?"

She reined in the horse, forcing a smile. "Eventful, Mr. Jennings. Very eventful."

"Ran into the Becketts, did you?" Casper chuckled. "They're good folk. Elijah can be a little particular about the ranch."

"Particular is one word for him," Molly replied, her tone dry. "Tell me, Mr. Jennings, is Elijah Beckett always so..."

"Prickly?" Casper finished, his eyes twinkling. "Only with folks he doesn't know. Or those he's taken an interest in."

Molly felt her cheeks warm. "I'm certain he hasn't taken an interest in me, Mr. Jennings. Unless you count wanting to run me off his property as interest."

Casper smiled, a hint of mischief in his weathered face. "Time will tell, Miss O'Sullivan. Time will tell."

"I'm going to unload my belongings and rest before supper, Mr. Jennings. It's been a long day."

As Molly continued to the hotel, Casper's words echoed in her mind. She'd come to Montana to capture the spirit of the frontier, not to get entangled with some mercurial rancher.

Back in her room at the Mystic Hotel, Molly unpacked her camera equipment, cleaning each item before repacking the box. She mentally listed what needed to be accomplished the following day.

After supper, she planned to set up her portable dark tent to develop the images she'd taken at the Beckett ranch. Tomorrow, she planned to deliver the best ones to Jolene, hoping Elijah would be gone.

Her fingers brushed against the wooden box, remembering how Elijah had almost grabbed it. His hands had been rough, calloused. A working man's hands. She then recalled how gentle those same hands were when they steadied Jolene.

Molly groaned, flopping onto the bed. She'd come west for adventure, for the opportunity to document the frontier with pictures. A rancher with steady green eyes and a determined nature wasn't going to distract her.

The following morning found Molly at the Golden Griddle. The hotel clerk had told her the widowed sisters who owned it made the best breakfasts in town. Savoring a bite of hotcakes, Molly had to agree the two women could cook.

Nursing a cup of coffee, she watched the happenings in town through the front window. Wagons and riders on horseback maneuvered along the main street. Inside, the restaurant buzzed with activity as customers filled up on eggs, potatoes, bacon, ham, and hotcakes while talking to tablemates or reading the paper. A copy had been left on her table, and Molly found it quite enjoyable.

"Are you finding the town interesting?" The gruff voice interrupted her reverie.

Molly looked up to see Sheriff Brodie Gaines standing by her table, his face creased with curiosity.

"Quite interesting. Would you care to join me?"

"Thank you. I need to get to the jail. Where have you been so far?"

"I took a buggy to the Beckett ranch yesterday. It's much larger than I imagined."

"It's impressive, all right. The family works hard to keep it profitable and growing. Someday, when Cody returns, they'll have one more experienced hand to help out."

"Cody?"

"He's the second oldest brother. Between Grayson and Elijah. Took off a few years ago when..." Brodie rubbed the back of his neck. "It's not my story to tell. Glad you got out there. It's worth the trip."

"Yes, it was..." she replied, though her thoughts were on the missing brother. "I hope to go one more time before moving on."

Brodie chuckled, tipping his hat. "Well, you picked a good time of year to come out. Weather's good, and most of the ranchers are busy breaking wild horses. Word is, there's going to be quite a commotion at the Beckett ranch later this week."

"Oh? What kind of commotion?"

"The boys are going to be breaking in a few horses. They've invited some neighbors to take part. It'll be a sight. Well, I'd best get going. You be careful wherever you head off to, Miss O'Sullivan."

As Brodie moved on, Molly thought of what he'd told her. This could be exactly the kind of authentic frontier moment she'd been hoping to capture.

She was still deliberating when the restaurant door burst open, and Nathan Beckett strode in, his face flushed with excitement.

"Molly!" he called out, spotting her. "Jolene told me to come fetch you. Josh is about to do something incredibly stupid, and I figured you'd want to get it on camera."

"I'm not sure going back today is such a good idea, Nathan. Your brother, Elijah—"

"Oh, don't worry about him." Nathan laughed, waving off her concern. "He rode off early to check on one of the herds."

As his enthusiasm washed over her, she felt her resolve weakening. This might be exactly the kind of moment she'd come to Montana to capture.

"All right. Let me grab my equipment and rent the buggy."

"No need for a buggy. I have a wagon right out front."

In less time than it took to butter a piece of toast, Molly was at the wagon with her equipment. Loading up, Josh secured the camera box, climbed onto the seat, and slapped the reins.

They rode along for several minutes before Molly spoke up.

"So, what exactly is Josh planning?"

Nathan's eyes twinkled with mischief. "He's got it in his head to break the new stallion we bought last week. Everyone says he's unrideable. Grayson told Ma he and Elijah would break him, taking their time. Well, Ma is still on her trip, Grayson rode off to Gumption to look at a bull, and Elijah is with a couple of our younger hands, tending to the herd in the far south quadrant. With all them gone, Josh has decided to give the rascal a try before any of them gets back."

Molly's eyebrows shot up. "And you think that's a good idea?"

"Heck no." Nathan chuckled. "But it'll make for a great show."

Chapter Six

As they passed the telegraph and post office, Titus Bell stepped out, calling to them. "Nathan. Hold up a moment!"

Nathan reined up the horses, and Titus approached, the usual creases of irritation on his face. "A letter came yesterday for you. It's actually for Naomi, so don't you be opening it."

Nathan slapped a hand over his heart. "You've got my word, Mr. Bell." Taking the letter from him, he noticed the corner of the man's mouth twitch. "Anything else?"

"That's all." Bell turned, stomping back into the office.

Molly felt Nathan stiffen beside her. "What is it?"

"The return address. It's from Cody." A hint of sadness laced his voice. Slapping the reins, the wagon lunged forward.

Crossing the town limits, Molly ventured a comment. "I heard he left a while back."

Nathan's knuckles whitened on the reins. "How

did you hear about him?"

"It doesn't matter."

He shook his head. "I guess not. He's the next oldest after Grayson. He's been gone a few years. His name doesn't come up much anymore. But Ma... I'm sure she thinks of him every day."

"I'm sure she does," Molly said softly.

"Maybe this letter will bring some good news." Nathan leaned back on the bench seat, his usual good humor absent. "Perhaps he's coming home."

Soon, the wagon rattled to a stop. Molly brimmed with anticipation as she took in the now familiar landscape. Then her gaze caught on two groups of people near a corral.

"Are you ready for some real Western action?" Nathan asked.

Her lips curved into a determined smile. "I certainly am."

Without hesitation, Molly hopped down from the wagon, her sturdy boots hitting the ground with a soft thud. She straightened her hat and smoothed her traveling outfit, then turned to Nathan with an expectant look.

"Where's the best spot for me to set up my camera? I want to capture every thrilling moment of this stallion breaking."

He grinned, pointing toward a spot near the corral. "Right over there should give you a perfect view. Are you sure you want to be close to the action? It can get pretty wild."

"I didn't come all the way to the ranch to watch

from the sidelines. I'm here to capture the true spirit of this wild land, danger and all."

As she spoke, Molly was already moving, her petite frame belying her strength as she hefted her camera equipment from the wagon. She strode toward the spot Nathan suggested, working at a fast clip to set everything up. Nathan stood beside her, curious as to all the different pieces of apparatus, before leaving to join Joshua and their youngest brother, Parker.

Molly's attention was suddenly drawn to a heated conversation between the three men. Parker Beckett's impatient voice cut through the air, his words sharp and clipped.

"Josh, this is crazy. That stallion's a killer. Besides, Grayson and Elijah were clear about us staying away from him."

Nathan chimed in, his usual upbeat tone tinged with worry. "Parker's right, Josh. It's not worth the risk. It would be best to wait for Grayson to decide when to break him."

Molly's hands stilled on her camera. She hadn't realized the stakes were so high. Her gaze darted between the brothers, taking in Nathan's concerned frown and Parker's tense stance.

Joshua stood before them, his tall frame relaxed despite the urgency in his brothers' voices. His light brown hair ruffled in the breeze as he regarded them calmly, a hint of a smile playing at the corners of his mouth.

"I appreciate your concern, boys," Joshua said, his

soft-spoken words carrying across the yard. "This is something I'm determined to do. The stallion has so much potential."

Parker threw up his hands in exasperation. "Potential? Josh, it's got the potential to stomp you into the ground."

Joshua's eyes sparkled with determination. "Maybe so. I've got a feeling about this one. Sometimes, you've got to take a chance to achieve something great."

Molly found herself drawn in by Joshua's quiet confidence. She'd seen many men bluster and boast, but there was something different about his calm resolve. It stirred a mix of admiration and anxiety within her.

"You sure about this, Josh?" Nathan asked, his voice softer now. "We can't afford to lose you, not with everything else going on."

Joshua placed a hand on Nathan's shoulder, his expression softening. "I'll be careful, I promise. Now, how about you two help me get ready instead of trying to talk me out of it?"

As the brothers moved toward the corral, Molly's enthusiasm began to fade. She'd come here expecting to capture a simple feat of horsemanship. Instead, she realized she might be witnessing something far more dangerous.

Her heart pounded as she watched Joshua, Nathan, and Parker enter the corral, their coiled ropes swinging loosely at their sides. The wild stallion snorted and pawed at the ground, its dark eyes glinting with defiance. Molly's knuckles whitened as she gripped her camera, her breath catching in her throat.

"Joshua Beckett, you get out of that corral this instant!" Jolene's voice rang out, sharp with concern. She strode toward the fence, her eyes flashing with a mix of anger and fear.

Lilian, the youngest Beckett sibling, hurried after her, her slight frame trembling. "Please, Josh. Listen to Jolene. It's not worth the risk."

Rebecca, the oldest of the two sisters, stopped beside Molly. "Josh is generally the most cautious of my brothers. His actions today make no sense."

Joshua turned to his sisters, a gentle smile on his face. "Ladies, I appreciate your concern, but this is something I need to do."

Jolene's jaw clenched. "Need to do? Or want to do to prove something?"

"Both, maybe," Joshua admitted, his gaze steady. "I've got Nathan and Parker here with me. We'll be careful."

Lilian wrung her hands. "What if something goes wrong? We can't lose you, Josh."

Molly found herself torn between her journalistic instincts and her growing concern for Joshua. She rose from her position of looking through the camera lens. "Is this really necessary?" she asked, surprised by the worry in her own voice.

Joshua's eyes met hers, and for a moment, Molly felt as if he could see right through her. "Sometimes, Miss O'Sullivan, the greatest tales come from taking risks."

His words struck a chord within her. Wasn't the unexpected why she'd come west in the first place? To find stories worth telling, even if it meant putting herself in unfamiliar, sometimes dangerous situations?

As the tension mounted, Molly realized she was witnessing more than just a man trying to break a horse. This was a family grappling with fear, love, and the pursuit of dreams. And at the center of it all stood Joshua, calm and resolute, ready to face whatever came next.

The stallion reared suddenly, its hooves slicing through the air...

Molly's chest tightened as she watched Joshua, Nathan, and Parker circling the stallion from inside the corral, their ropes at the ready. Her fingers hovered over her camera's shutter, but a nagging doubt crept into her mind. Was she really prepared to capture potentially devastating images?

Joshua's voice cut through her thoughts. "Easy now, boy," he coaxed, inching closer to the stallion.

Molly's grip tightened on her camera. "If something goes wrong..." she whispered, her stomach churning.

Just then, Joshua made his move. With lightning speed, he swung his rope, and it sailed through the air. Time seemed to slow as the loop descended toward the stallion's head.

"You've got him," Parker shouted.

Before either Nathan or Parker could throw their

ropes, a sharp yell pierced the air, followed by two deafening gunshots. Molly whirled around, her heart pounding in her ears.

Molly's eyes widened as she saw Elijah Beckett and three younger men on horseback thunder toward them. The tension in the air thickened, electric and dangerous.

"We're in for it now," Jolene exclaimed, her voice tight with worry.

Molly's grip on her camera tightened as she studied Elijah's face, set in grim determination. His eyes blazed with intensity, sending a shiver down her spine.

As the riders drew closer, Molly could make out the faces of the other men. No boys, she realized. They couldn't be more than fourteen or fifteen. Though young, their expressions mirrored Elijah's stern features, and Molly's stomach knotted with apprehension.

Rebecca stepped closer to Molly, her voice low and urgent. "This won't be good. Eli and Gray were firm in their orders for no one to approach the stallion."

Molly nodded, her instincts kicking in despite her growing unease. Whatever was coming, it was big enough to interrupt Joshua's attempt with the stallion.

She glanced back at the corral, where he still held the rope around the stallion's neck, his face a mask of resignation and growing irritation. Nathan and Parker had moved to flank him, their stances protective.

Molly squared her shoulders, lifting her chin as she always did when facing a challenge. She wouldn't allow herself to cower before the intensity of Elijah Beckett.

"Miss O'Sullivan," Elijah called out as he reined his horse to a stop and dismounted. "I believe it's time for you to leave." His voice, clipped and terse, had her stiffen.

She felt her temper flare. "I beg your pardon. I'm here at the invitation of your brother and sister-in-law."

His jaw tightened. "This is family business. You won't want to witness what may happen next."

"I'm not some delicate flower to be shooed away at the first sign of trouble, Mr. Beckett."

As the tension mounted, Molly wondered what exactly might happen next.

Joshua loosened the rope around the horse's neck, letting it drop to the ground as the stallion dashed away. Nathan and Parker exchanged a quick glance before stepping closer to Joshua, their bodies taut with tension.

"Eli," Joshua called out, his soft voice carrying a hint of steel.

Elijah's eyes flashed as he strode toward the corral. "Breaking the stallion isn't your job, Josh. Besides, we've got bigger problems."

Parker snorted, his impatience getting the better of him. "What type of problems?"

"Rustlers," Elijah spat, the word suspended in the

air between them. "They hit the south pasture sometime in the last two days."

Joshua's grip on the now coiled rope slackened. "How many?"

"At least fifty head," Elijah replied. "Maybe more."

Parker blew out a breath, his earlier bravado replaced by a grim resolve. "Who would dare?"

Elijah's gaze swept over his brothers, landing on Molly. His expression hardened. "That's what we need to find out. And we can't do that with... distractions."

Molly bristled at the implication. "I'm not leaving, Mr. Beckett. This is something people, unaware of these issues, would be interested in learning about."

Joshua intervened, his calm voice a stark contrast to the tension surrounding them. "Leave her be, Eli."

Elijah's nostrils flared, a battle raging behind his eyes. The stallion, sensing the discord, blew loudly and stomped its hooves.

Then, with a barely perceptible nod, Elijah relented, knowing they had to focus on the missing cattle and not on a city woman out of place on the ranch.

Before he could respond, a distant rumble of hoofbeats echoed across the ranch. All eyes turned toward the sound, a new wave of tension washing over the group.

"Riders coming," Parker muttered, his hand now firmly on his pistol.

Molly's heart lurched as she watched the Beckett brothers form a protective line in front of the women.

The thundering hoofbeats grew louder, dust billowing on the horizon as a group of riders approached. The Beckett brothers stood shoulder to shoulder, a united front against the possible threat.

Recognizing the lead rider, Elijah's voice cut through the tension. "Relax, boys. It's the sheriff. It looks like Jubal Whitton and Tripp Lassiter are with him." He was surprised to see Deputy Whitton and their friend, Tripp, riding with him.

The broad-shouldered man Molly had spoken with earlier at breakfast reined in his horse a few yards from where they stood.

"Eli," Sheriff Gaines called out. "We need to talk."

Chapter Seven

Elijah stepped forward, his posture taut as a drawn bowstring. "Brodie. Jubal. Tripp. To what do we owe the pleasure?"

The three men dismounted, handing their reins to the younger boys who worked for the Becketts. "Tripp has some cattle missing. You noticed any trouble?"

Elijah shifted uneasily. "We sure have. At least fifty of our cattle are missing. We were just about to ride out to find them." He looked at Tripp. "How many?"

"Same as you. About fifty head." Tripp's gaze swept over the group, lingering on Molly for a moment before returning to Elijah.

"Any other ranchers affected?" Elijah asked.

"None who've come to me," Brodie replied. "My guess is between you and Tripp, they've gotten all they can handle for now. They're probably close to the Wyoming border by now."

Tripp broke the silence, his voice tight. "Maybe not. Depends on the number of rustlers involved. I want to go after them."

"I'm with you, Tripp. It would have to be me, Joshua, and Nathan. We need the others to stay here."

"The three of you are good. I'll bring two men, so we'll have six."

"Now, hold up a minute," Brodie said. "I don't want a killing spree."

Nathan sent a disbelieving look at the sheriff. "Hard to prevent it when they've stolen our cattle."

"You don't need to come with us, Brodie." Elijah shot a look at Tripp, who nodded. "Might be better if you didn't."

The sheriff nodded. "Don't see how I can. Beaumont is up in Helena. His ma is sick. So it's just Jubal and me."

"We'll do our best to keep the killing to a minimum," Tripp said. "Maybe we'll be able to drive the herd back this way without them knowing."

Brodie sent him a dubious glance. "I'd pay money to see that." He blew out a breath. "Bring back any bodies."

"Will do," Elijah answered. "What else is bothering you, Brodie?"

The sheriff sighed, removing his hat to wipe his brow. "There's talk of a new gang moving into the territory from the Dakotas. They've been causing havoc up north. I'm afraid they might set their sights on Mystic." Brodie looked around at the gathering and cleared his throat. "They aren't our usual outlaws who rob banks or steal cattle. Instead, they swindle unsuspecting people of their savings or title to their homes. The swindlers destroy lives the same as a shot to the heart."

Joshua rubbed his stubbled jaw. "Mystic would be a ripe target for those inscrutable thieves."

Elijah's expression darkened. "How's that?"

"I'm not worried about you or Tripp," Brodie said. "You'd never let someone take away what's yours with a signature. They're a loose gang, of sorts. Organized and ruthless when it comes to who they target. An older widow or widower who has money is their favorite."

Jolene couldn't contain herself any longer. "Those poor people. What can we do, Sheriff?"

"I'm alerting everyone in Mystic to be aware of the swindles going on in other territories. Pastor Ward has agreed to make an announcement during church this Sunday. Mayor Jurgen is having flyers made to post around town. Him being a widower, he's determined nothing unsavory will happen in Mystic. Titus Bell is going to make sure the stage drivers know to warn riders of the danger. I'm open to any ideas you folks have."

Molly thought a moment. "I don't know any of the people who live outside of town. Well, besides the Becketts and Mr. Lassiter. If I'm given names and locations, I can take the buggy and warn them."

"What a wonderful idea, Molly. We'll take one of our wagons and ride out this week," Jolene said.

"That isn't going to happen," Elijah said. "Grayson will never let you go in your condition."

"But—"

"I'll go with Molly," Annalee offered. "I won't need names or directions, as I know everyone for miles around Mystic."

"I'd appreciate it, Annie," Brodie said, his voice soft.

Molly watched as Annalee's face grew red. She wondered if there might be something going on between the sheriff and Annalee.

Brodie tore his gaze from hers before clearing his throat. "All right. Jubal and I need to get back to town." He looked at Tripp. "When are you riding out?"

"Within the hour, if Elijah will be ready."

"We'll ride back to your ranch with you, Tripp, and head out from there."

"Don't you want to wait for Grayson to return?" Jolene asked.

"He may not get back for a few more hours. We need to find our cattle before dark," Elijah said.

As Elijah and Tripp began to outline their plan, a chill ran down Molly's spine. She'd come to Wild Spirit Ranch seeking a story about the wild frontier. Instead, she found two families dealing with rustlers, and swindlers who could land in Mystic at any time.

Grayson arrived back at the ranch two hours after Elijah, Joshua, and Nathan rode with Tripp to Iron

Angel Ranch. He'd been held up in Gumption when the owner of the bull he hoped to buy had tripped over a pitchfork. His wife patched him up, though it took almost an hour before negotiations resumed.

Molly had been invited to stay for supper with those left at the ranch. It was somewhat of a celebration, as Grayson and the Gumption rancher had come to an agreement for the bull to become part of Wild Spirit Ranch.

"We'll fetch him later this week," Grayson said. "Gumption may be a small town, but they know how to raise prime bulls."

After supper, Molly helped the Beckett women clean the dishes before excusing herself for the ride back to Mystic.

"Nonsense," Jolene said. "You'll stay with us tonight."

"I don't want to intrude."

"You won't be. We have two empty guest rooms. You may pick which one you want." Jolene hung a kitchen towel on a hook. "If I'm not mistaken, Elijah has an extra nightshirt you could wear."

"Elijah?" The horror on Molly's face had the women laughing.

"No? Then I suppose you'll have to wear one of mine." Jolene continued to chuckle.

Feeling her face flush, she allowed herself to be drawn into the joke. "I do believe one of your nightgowns would be best. Thank you."

An hour later, Molly sat in one of the guest rooms, finishing an entry in her journal. Setting it aside, she grabbed a shawl. Jolene had already gone to bed, exhausted after such a long day.

Molly walked down the stairs, not yet sleepy enough to retire. She wanted to see the area around the barns, house, and corrals at night.

Stepping out onto the porch, she tightened the shawl around her. It continued to surprise her how chilly the nights could be when the days were almost too warm. The almost full moon allowed her to see a great deal.

Taking the steps to the ground, she strolled to the closest corral, watching as two colts played under the moonlight. They were so carefree, with nothing to intrude on their fun.

Suddenly, a bloodcurdling scream pierced the air, causing everyone to freeze. It came from the direction of the main house.

"Jolene!" Grayson's face went pale as he bolted out of the barn and ran toward the house, Parker on his heels.

Molly hesitated for a split second before rushing after them. Pounding up the steps, she followed them upstairs, coming to a stop in the hall.

Another sharp cry pierced the air of the Beckett homestead, echoing through the rafters of the ranch house. Jolene, her face contorted in pain, clutched her swollen belly as she braced herself against the doorframe of the bedroom.

"It's time," she gasped, her eyes wide with a mixture of fear and pain. "The baby's coming!"

Grayson, ever the protective husband, was at her side in an instant, his strong arms supporting her trembling frame. His calm expression cracked, revealing a flicker of panic in his intense eyes.

"Now? But it's too early," he muttered, his voice tight with concern.

Annalee Beckett, always quick to take charge, sprang into action. "Lilian, fetch some warm water from downstairs. Molly, I need you to grab a stack of clean cotton from the wardrobe in the hall."

As Lilian darted out of the room, her petite form disappearing down the staircase, Molly hesitated, her eyes wide with a mix of curiosity and apprehension.

"Have you helped with a birth before?" she asked Annalee.

"First time. Guess we don't have much choice."

Parker, the youngest Beckett sibling, hovered uncertainly near the door. "What should I do?" he asked, his impatience evident in his clipped tone.

Grayson, still supporting Jolene, shot his brother a stern look. "Stay calm and be ready to help if we need you."

Jolene let out another pained groan, her fingers digging into Grayson's arm. "I don't care who does what," she managed through gritted teeth. "Just get this baby out of me!"

The tension in the room was palpable as Lilian

returned, carefully balancing a basin of steaming water. Molly followed close behind, her arms laden with soft cloths.

Annalee's voice was steady and reassuring. "All right, let's get Jolene comfortable on the bed. Grayson, help her lie down."

As they maneuvered Jolene onto the bed, she locked eyes with her husband. "Grayson," she whispered, a hint of fear creeping into her voice, "what if something goes wrong?"

His face softened. "Nothing's going to go wrong, darlin'," he murmured, his voice low and soothing. "You're the strongest woman I know. This is just another adventure for us."

Jolene managed a weak smile, drawing strength from his words and the love shining in his eyes. As another contraction seized her, she couldn't help but wonder if this would be an adventure with a happy ending.

Chapter Eight

Annalee surveyed the room, her gaze sharp and determined. She squared her shoulders, channeling the same resolve she used when facing down a stubborn steer.

"Grayson and Parker. I need you both to head downstairs now. We've got things under control here."

Grayson hesitated, his broad frame tensing as he looked from Annalee to Jolene. "Are you sure? I don't want to leave her—"

"She'll be fine," Annalee interrupted, her tone softening. "We'll take good care of her, I promise. We need space to work, and you'll only be in the way."

Parker, already inching toward the door, nodded with vigor. "Come on, Gray. Annie knows what she's doing." He tugged at his older brother's arm, eager to escape the tense atmosphere.

Grayson leaned down, pressing a gentle kiss to Jolene's forehead. "I'll be right downstairs if you need me," he murmured, his clipped tone filled with tenderness.

As the men left the room, Molly stepped forward, her eyes wide with a mixture of curiosity and concern.

Annalee's confidence faltered for a moment as she met Molly's inquiring gaze. She took a deep breath, her slim frame straightening.

"Ma was supposed to be here for this." Her eyes flickered with quiet resolve. "But she's still gone, and we can't very well ask this little one to wait, can we?"

Jolene let out a pained groan, her gaze locking onto Annalee's. "I trust you, Annie," she managed through gritted teeth, her hair plastered to her forehead with sweat.

Annalee nodded. "All right, ladies, we may not have experience, but we're going to bring this baby into the world. That's the Beckett way, after all." She glanced at Lilian and Molly. "We'll do this just like women have been doing since time began."

Lilian, her face somewhat pale, stepped forward. "I've helped birth calves. Can't be too different, right?"

Annalee couldn't help chuckling. "All right, Jolene. You're strong and brave. You left behind a life of luxury in Savannah to build a home here with Grayson. If you can do that, you can do this."

Jolene nodded, a ghost of a smile flickering across her face despite the pain. "I wouldn't trade this life for anything."

As another contraction hit, Annalee looked at Molly. "Support her head and shoulders. Lilian, get ready with those cloths." She positioned herself at the foot of the bed, her heart thundering but her voice steady. "All right, Jolene. When I say push, you give it everything you've got."

The next hour passed in a blur of activity, punctuated by Jolene's screams and the encouraging words of the women around her. Annalee found herself drawing on every ounce of knowledge she possessed, guiding Jolene through each push with a calm she didn't entirely feel.

Finally, with one last monumental effort from Jolene, a new cry filled the room. Annalee's hands trembled slightly as she cradled the squalling infant, a boy with a shock of dark hair, just like his father's.

"You did it, Jolene," Annalee said, her voice thick with emotion as she wrapped the baby in a clean cloth. "He's perfect."

As she placed the newborn in Jolene's arms, Annalee felt a surge of pride and love wash over her. This was what it meant to be part of the Beckett family, to face challenges and emerge victorious.

Annalee opened her mouth to ask Jolene about a name for the baby when the door burst open. Naomi Beckett, her graying brown hair windswept, strode into the room with the energy of a woman half her age.

"I'm not too late, am I?" Naomi's voice, direct as ever, filled the space.

Annalee's eyes widened in surprise. "Mama! We thought you were still on your trip."

Naomi's gaze softened as it fell on Jolene and the

newborn. "Couldn't stay away when I knew my first grandchild was on the way."

Jolene, exhausted but beaming, looked up at her mother-in-law. "You're just in time to meet your grandson."

Naomi moved closer, her petite frame belying the strength garnered through decades of ranch life. She peered down at the baby, a smile softening her stern features.

"Well, now," she said, her voice uncharacteristically gentle. "Isn't he something?"

Lilian practically bounced with excitement. "He's perfect, Mama."

Naomi chuckled, patting Lilian's shoulder. "Yes, he is perfect."

Molly watched the scene unfold, feeling warmth spread through her chest. This wasn't just the birth of a child. It was the continuation of their family legacy. Feeling like the outsider she was, she made her way to the door.

"So," Naomi said, her tone shifting back to its usual businesslike manner, "what are we calling this little cowboy?"

"Well," Jolene began hesitantly, "Grayson and I had talked about naming him after his absent brother."

Naomi's breath caught. "You mean... Cody?"

Jolene nodded, her eyes glistening. "Cody Grayson Beckett. What do you think?"

For a moment, the room was silent, save for the soft coos of the baby. Then Naomi spoke, her voice thick with emotion. "I think it's a wonderful name."

As the women gathered around, marveling at little Cody and celebrating his arrival, Jolene looked at Naomi. "Do you want to get Grayson?"

"I certainly would." A few seconds later, Naomi's voice rang out from the top of the stairs. "Grayson. It's time for you to meet your son."

The aroma of spice cake wafted through the Beckett family kitchen, mingling with the earthy scent of strong coffee. Naomi Beckett's keen eyes settled on the unfamiliar young woman seated at her dining table. Her gaze flickered between the stranger and her daughter, Annalee, a mixture of curiosity and skepticism playing across her lined features.

"Well, now," Naomi drawled, her voice carrying the weight of years on the Montana frontier. "Who might this young lady be, Annalee? Don't tell me you've gone and adopted another stray."

Molly O'Sullivan's cheeks flushed, her eyes widening at the matriarch's blunt assessment. She opened her mouth to speak, but Annalee's laughter cut through the air.

"Oh, Mama." Annalee chuckled. "You know I can't resist a lost soul. But I promise, this one's just visiting."

Naomi's eyebrow arched. "Is that so? And what brings a city girl like yourself out to our little slice of heaven, Miss...?"

"O'Sullivan, ma'am. Molly O'Sullivan. I'm a photographer from Chicago. I've come to capture the beauty of Montana."

Naomi snorted, a sound somewhere between amusement and disbelief. "Beauty, is it? Well, I suppose there's still some beauty out here, if you don't mind incredibly difficult, backbreaking work and calluses to go with it."

Molly laughed, her nervousness melting away. "I assure you, Mrs. Beckett, I'm not afraid of hard work. Or cow manure, either."

Naomi chuckled, her earlier skepticism softening, if only a little.

"Oh, there's plenty of beauty here," Annalee insisted. "You should see the sunset over Moon River, Molly. It's as if angels painted the sky."

Molly grinned, imagining the scene Annalee described. "I'd love to see it. In fact, I'd love to photograph all of Wild Spirit Ranch."

Annalee nodded. "That's why Jolene invited Molly to stay for supper and the night, Ma. She thought Molly could get some good shots tomorrow, maybe even of the boys working the herd."

Naomi's eyebrows shot up. "I see."

"You know Jolene wouldn't invite anyone who wasn't trustworthy," Annalee said.

Naomi sighed. "I suppose you're right. Well, Miss O'Sullivan, it seems you'll be joining us for breakfast tomorrow."

Molly grinned, her earlier trepidation forgotten.

"I'm happy to help, Mrs. Beckett. And please, call me Molly."

Lilian, who'd been silent, offered a slow smile before taking a sip of her tepid coffee. Beside her, Parker took the last bite of cake while looking between his mother and Molly.

He opened his mouth to speak but stopped at the sound of the front door opening. Elijah, Joshua, and Nathan strode in, their boots caked with mud and their faces etched with exhaustion.

Annalee jumped up, her earlier mirth replaced by excitement. "Oh, you're just in time. We have wonderful news. Jolene just had their baby. A little boy. They named him Cody Grayson Beckett."

The brothers' faces transformed, weariness giving way to joy. Joshua grinned while Nathan let out a whoop of delight. Even Elijah's expression softened, a ghost of a smile playing at his lips.

As Annalee filled them in on the details, Molly found herself slipping away to the kitchen. She wasn't sure why, but something compelled her to let the family members have time to themselves.

She wanted to make herself useful. Perhaps it was the ingrained hospitality her mother had instilled in her, or maybe it was a desire to show her gratitude for the Becketts' kindness.

Molly busied herself preparing plates of the cake Lilian had baked earlier and pouring cups of strong, black coffee. As she worked, she could hear the continued chatter from the other room, punctuated by Elijah's deep, rumbling voice. Despite their rocky start, she found herself drawn to his voice, wondering how it would sound if he ever decided to laugh.

Molly stepped into the dining room, the tray holding the cake and cups of coffee balanced carefully in her hands. She approached the table where Elijah, Joshua, and Nathan sat. Their conversation hushed as she drew near, three pairs of eyes turning to watch her.

"I thought you gentlemen might appreciate some food," Molly said, her voice steady despite the slight tremor in her hands. She set a plate and cup in front of Joshua first, who offered a broad smile.

"That's mighty kind of you, Molly. Thank you," Joshua said, his soft-spoken tone genuine.

Nathan's face lit up as Molly placed his portion before him. "Thank you, Molly."

Finally, she reached Elijah. The eldest Beckett brother's gaze met hers for a brief moment before flicking away. As she set down his plate and cup, he merely grunted, not bothering to look up again.

She felt a flash of irritation at his brusque manner. Instead, she pushed it aside, recalling how she'd dealt with pricklier malcontents during her photography career in Chicago. If Elijah Beckett thought his silence would intimidate her, he was mistaken.

As Molly turned to leave, Naomi's voice rang out. "Now, don't you dare think about slinking off, young lady. Come sit down and join us. The boys were just going to talk about the rustlers."

Molly hesitated, caught between her desire to give the family privacy and her curiosity about the recent events. Naomi's stern expression brooked no argument, so Molly found herself settling into a chair next to Nathan.

"Now then," Naomi continued, her eyes sharp as she surveyed her sons. "Go ahead and tell us about the rustlers."

Joshua leaned forward, his calm appearance tinged with excitement. "Nathan already told you Tripp and his men were with us. We tracked them to Black Canyon. Elijah's hunch about Flatrock being their hideout was right."

Elijah's face was impassive as he sipped his coffee.

"We managed to catch them off guard." Nathan's voice brimmed with pride. "Tripp came up with a brilliant plan to distract them while the rest of us rounded up the cattle."

Molly found herself leaning in, captivated by the tale. She glanced at Elijah, noticing the way his jaw clenched when his gaze met hers.

Joshua cleared his throat, his expression turning serious. "We need to inform Brodie about what happened. Those rustlers won't take kindly to losing the cattle after all they did to steal them."

"I reckon they might try to retaliate." Nathan stuffed the last bite of cake into his mouth.

A tense silence fell over the room. Molly felt a chill run down her spine as she considered the implications. She'd come to Mystic seeking adventure, but she hadn't bargained for this level of danger.

Elijah suddenly spoke, his voice low and gravelly. "I'll ride into town at first light to speak with Brodie.

We need to be prepared for whatever comes next."

"I'll go with you, Eli," Joshua said. "I want to let Faith know what happened."

Naomi snorted. "Why would the newspaper editor want to run an article on our troubles? She has no interest in what happens with ranchers."

"Mama," Annalee said, sending an understanding look at Joshua. "Faith Goodell is fair in her reporting. It's just the townsfolk have more going on for her to write about. The ranchers keep to themselves and aren't prone to talking about their lives. I think she'd want to include an article about rustlers in the next paper."

Naomi rose, stifling a yawn behind her hand. "You do what you think best, Joshua. I'm going to check on my new grandson, then go to bed."

The rest of the family continued to talk after Naomi left. Molly couldn't help wondering what she'd gotten herself into. Wild Spirit Ranch was proving to be far more than a picturesque backdrop for her photographs.

Chapter Nine

One by one, the Becketts began to disperse, heading to their respective bedrooms. Molly lingered for a moment at the table, gathering the dishes and taking them to the kitchen. As she made her way up the stairs, she couldn't help feeling Elijah's gaze on her back. Closing the door behind her, she rested against it, releasing a slow breath.

At the top of the landing, Elijah paused outside Molly's door. His hand hovered to knock, an unfamiliar conflict brewing within him. He'd spent the last couple hours sneaking glances at her, noticing the way her eyes lit up when listening to them discuss the rustlers, the gentle curve of her smile when the family joked among themselves.

Drawing his hand back, he ran it through his thick hair. He was beginning to enjoy her company, and the realization unsettled him more than he cared to admit.

The door opening had him taking a step back. Molly stood there, looking at him with a curious stare. "Elijah? Is everything all right?"

He cleared his throat, caught off guard. "Yeah," he managed, his usual gruffness softened by a hint of uncertainty. "You?"

"I'm fine, thank you," Molly replied, a smile evident in her voice. "Goodnight, Elijah."

"Night," he grunted, turning away. As he strode toward his room, Elijah's thoughts were on the city girl who'd stumbled into his life. She was becoming more than just an inconvenience. Molly O'Sullivan was becoming a distraction he wasn't sure he could afford.

Molly poured herself a cup of coffee the following morning, taking a sip before approaching Naomi Beckett. The older woman stood at the sink, her slender hands immersed in soapy water as she scrubbed a deep pot with practiced efficiency.

Molly took a deep breath, clutching the cup with both hands. "Mrs. Beckett." Her voice was tinged with trepidation. "I was wondering if I might speak with you about something."

Naomi glanced up, her eyes sharp and assessing. "What is it, Molly?" she asked, her tone direct but not unkind.

Molly stepped closer. "I've been thinking about the younger boys at Wild Spirit Ranch. I find myself incredibly curious about them. I overheard Annabell and Lilian referring to them as orphans. I was hoping... well, I was wondering if I might be able to extend my stay here. Just for a little while longer."

Naomi's eyebrows rose, her hands stilling in the cooling water. "Extend your stay? For what purpose?"

Molly's words tumbled out in a rush. "I'd like to document their stories. Through my photography and some interviews. These boys, they've been through so much, and I believe their experiences deserve to be captured, to be remembered."

Naomi remained silent for a moment, her gaze fixed on Molly. The young woman could almost see the thoughts churning behind those weathered eyes, weighing the pros and cons of her request.

After a time, Naomi spoke, her voice measured. "Molly, this is a working ranch, not a curiosity shop. These boys have chores and responsibilities. Their time isn't to be frittered away posing for pictures."

Molly's heart sank. She pressed on, her innate stubbornness rising to the surface. "I understand. I promise I won't interfere with their duties. I'll work around their schedules, be as unobtrusive as possible. Please, I truly believe this could be something meaningful, not just for me, but for them as well."

Naomi sighed, wiping her hands on her apron. She looked out the window, her gaze sweeping over the vast expanse of the ranch. When she turned back to Molly, there was a hint of softness in her eyes.

"You're a determined young woman, aren't you?" A ghost of a smile touched her lips. "All right. You can stay on one condition. You pull your weight around here. I won't have you being a burden on this household."

"Oh, thank you, Naomi. I won't be a burden. I'll help with whatever needs doing, you have my word."

Naomi nodded. "See you do. And you'll tell Elijah what you're doing. He's the one closest to the orphans. Now, if you'll excuse me, I have work to attend to."

As Naomi turned back to the sink, Molly finished her coffee and hurried outside. She needed to find Elijah and explain this new development. Perhaps seek his advice. Despite his aloof nature, she found herself drawn to the taciturn rancher.

The sun beat down mercilessly on Elijah's broad shoulders as he mended a section of fence near the barn, his muscled arms working with practiced efficiency. Sweat glistened on his brow, and he paused to wipe it away with the back of his hand, leaving a smudge of dirt across his forehead.

Molly approached, her breath catching at the image he made. A testimony to the intensely physical work required on a ranch.

"Elijah!" Her voice brimmed with barely contained excitement.

He looked up, his eyes narrowing at the interruption. "Molly," he replied, his tone curt.

Molly reached the fence, her cheeks flushed from

the combination of the heat and her enthusiasm. "I have news to share," she began, her words tumbling out in a rush. "I've spoken with Naomi, and she's agreed to let me stay on at the ranch a while longer. I want to document the lives of the boys here through photographs and interviews."

Elijah's jaw tightened, his expression skeptical. "That so? And what exactly do you aim to accomplish?"

She chose her words with care. "The boys must have incredible stories. Their resilience, their strength. It deserves to be captured, to be shared with the world. I want to show people the heart of Wild Spirit Ranch, the difference it's making in these young lives."

As she spoke, he found himself studying her face, noting the determination in her eyes, the genuine care in her voice. It was somewhat unsettling how her enthusiasm seemed to chip away at his impassive pose.

"It's not going to be easy. These boys, they've been through a lot. They might not want to open up to a stranger."

"I understand. I'm willing to put in the time to earn their trust. I believe in the importance of sharing their stories. Will you help me?"

Elijah hesitated, his internal struggle evident in the set of his jaw. Part of him wanted to dismiss the idea outright. He had work to do, after all, and this was a distraction. Something in Molly's earnest gaze gave him pause.

"I'll consider it. My priority is the ranch and the boys' well-being. Those come first, understood?"

Molly's face broke into a radiant smile, catching him off guard. "Of course," she agreed readily. "Thank you, Elijah. I promise you won't regret this."

As she turned to leave, her steps light with excitement, Elijah found himself watching her go, a strange mix of emotions stirring in his chest. What had he just agreed to? And why did he have the unsettling feeling his carefully ordered world was about to be turned upside down?

The following morning, Elijah found Molly in the kitchen, talking with Annalee. They were in a conversation about baby Beckett, and how Jolene and Grayson had decided to name him Cody Grayson.

He approached with measured steps, his expression neutral despite the unexpected flutter in his chest at the sight of her.

"Mornin'. You're up early, Molly."

"Couldn't sleep. I'm excited about meeting the boys and hearing their stories."

Elijah nodded. "We'll start with the youngest."

As they walked, Molly fell into step beside him. "Tell me about him."

Elijah's voice was low and steady. "His name is Gavin. He's twelve. I found him hiding in our barn last winter, half-starved and scared out of his wits."

"What happened to him?"

"Parents died in a fire," Elijah replied, his jaw tightening. "He'd been on his own for months, just trying to survive."

They approached a boy brushing down a pony, his movements gentle and methodical.

"Gavin," Elijah called softly. "Come meet Miss O'Sullivan."

He looked up, wariness evident in his eyes.

Molly smiled. "Hello, Gavin. That's a beautiful pony you've got there."

Gavin nodded shyly. "She's a mare. Her name's Daisy."

As Molly engaged him in conversation, Elijah watched, a mix of surprise and admiration rising within him. He'd expected the boy to shy away, but Molly's gentle character seemed to put him at ease.

Elijah busied himself inside the barn while keeping watch on them. It had taken months for Gavin to open up to him. No telling how long it would take for the boy to be comfortable with Molly. An hour passed before Molly joined him.

"It's a remarkable story. We're going to talk again tomorrow."

"Do you want to talk to another of the orphans?"

She cleared her throat, an edge of distress in her voice. "Yes, I would."

Elijah led Molly toward the corral on the other side of the barn, where an older boy was working with a beautiful colt. They stopped, resting their arms on the top rung of the fence.

"That's Samuel. He's sixteen. His ma died and his pa was a mean drunk. Samuel ran away after a bad beating. He ended up at the door of the orphanage in town. They didn't have any beds, so they brought him out here."

Molly's face clouded with empathy. "How awful. These boys have been through so much."

"Life isn't always kind out here. These boys are survivors, every one of them."

When Samuel finished, he walked the colt toward them. "Hey, Eli."

"Samuel, this is Miss O'Sullivan."

"I've seen her around the ranch. She's the one with the camera."

"Right. How about I take care of the colt, and you have a chat with Miss O'Sullivan?"

Samual shrugged, handing the lead rope to Elijah. "I guess so."

Molly and Samuel talked for several minutes before she found Elijah inside the barn. "Samuel has been through a great deal. We're going to talk again tomorrow or the next day."

As they continued their tour, Elijah shared not just the boys' stories but his own observations and feelings about each of them. Molly listened, her questions thoughtful and perceptive.

By midday, they'd met most of the boys, and Elijah was surprised to find himself feeling lighter, as if sharing the weight of these stories had somehow eased his own burden.

"Thank you, Elijah," Molly said softly as they

paused near the corral. "For taking the time to introduce me to those extraordinary boys."

Elijah met her gaze, struck by the depth of understanding he saw there. For a moment, he allowed himself to imagine what life might be like if...

Then reality reasserted itself, and he cleared his throat. "You should head back to the house. I've got work to finish up."

As he walked away, Molly knew each boy's story affected Elijah deeply. He might show the world a tough as leather exterior, but inside, he had a big, warm heart.

Chapter Ten

Molly carefully adjusted her tripod early in the morning two days later. Bending, she looked through the lens of her camera, poised to capture the essence of the boys' lives.

"All right, Samuel," Molly called out. "Stand there by the barn door. Yes. That's good."

He shifted from foot to foot. "Miss Molly, I've never had my picture taken."

Straightening away from her camera, she offered him a reassuring smile. "There's nothing to worry about. Tell me, what's your favorite part of working on the ranch?"

As Samuel's face lit up, Molly quickly bent down again to look through the lens, capturing the genuine enthusiasm on the boy's face.

"I guess it's working with the horses," he replied, his posture relaxing. "There's this one mare, Starlight. She's got a fierce temper, but she's startin' to warm up to me."

Molly quickly exchanged plates and took another

image. "That's wonderful. How did you manage to gain her trust?"

As he launched into his tale, Molly changed plates and took one more photograph, her keen eye catching the subtle shift in his expression. When developed, she knew the image would show the pride in his accomplishments, as well as the lingering uncertainty of a boy forced to grow up too fast.

"You know, Miss Molly, before I came here, I never thought I'd amount to much. My pa, he..." His voice trailed off, eyes clouding with painful memories.

She gave him her full attention. "It's all right, Samuel. You don't have to share anything you're not comfortable with."

He swallowed hard. "Pa always said I was good for nothing. But here, with the Becketts and the other boys, I'm startin' to think maybe he was wrong."

Molly felt a lump form in her throat, touched by the boy's vulnerability. "I want you to know something. The way you've connected with Starlight takes patience and kindness. Those are rare qualities, and they make you very special indeed."

Over the next few hours, Molly worked her way through the ranch, photographing and interviewing each of the boys. With every story she heard, her admiration for these resilient young souls grew. Each boy had a unique tale, a testament to their strength and the second chance Wild Spirit Ranch had given them.

Later in the afternoon, Molly developed the plates

in a room with only one small window, which she covered with a thick blanket. As the images came to life, she felt a tear running down her cheek. She'd captured the heart of each boy.

As the sun dipped below the horizon, Molly found herself sitting on the porch steps with Elijah. In her hand, she held images of each boy. One at a time, she handed them to Elijah.

He studied each one. "These are good, Molly." Going through them again, he handed them back. "You did good by them."

"I can't thank you enough for this opportunity." Her voice was filled with genuine gratitude. "These boys, their stories… they're incredible."

He nodded, his expression softened by the fading light. "They're good boys, all of them. They just needed a chance to prove it."

"Elijah, how do you do it? Carry the weight of all their pasts, their hopes?"

He was silent for a long moment, his gaze fixed on the distant mountains. "Truth is, some days, I wonder if we're doing a good job."

"You and your family are doing more than you realize. Those boys deserve a decent chance in life, and you're providing it. Don't ever doubt how much the boys appreciate what they have here."

Late the next afternoon, Elijah shoveled loose hay

into the press used to make small bales. Parker helped by pulling out the finished bales and stacking them. It was a process, and it strained their muscles. The reward came when all the bales were stacked and easier to move by wagon to far reaches of the ranch.

From Elijah's vantage point, he could see Molly seated on a weathered wooden crate, listening to one of young Gavin's animated tales.

Pausing, he swiped sweat from his brow with the back of his hand. He'd been skeptical of Molly's project at first, but watching her now, he couldn't deny the genuine interest in her eyes. She nodded, encouraging Gavin as he spoke.

"Sounds to me you showed the ornery steer who's boss, didn't you?" Her laughter carried on the evening breeze, warm and infectious.

Gavin beamed, chest puffing with pride. "Yes, ma'am. Elijah says I'm a natural with the lasso now."

Elijah's lips twitched in a rare smile. He'd never seen the boys so eager to share their stories. Molly had a way of drawing them out, making them feel heard and valued.

As if sensing his gaze, Molly glanced up, meeting Elijah's gaze. She offered a slight wave, and he found himself nodding in acknowledgment before returning to his task.

"Eli!" Joshua's voice rang out as he approached on

horseback early the following morning. "I'm heading into town to meet with Miss Goodell. Need anything while I'm there?"

Elijah shook his head. "We're set here. How long will you be?"

Joshua dismounted, a faint smile playing on his lips. "Oh, I expect I'll be back before supper. Just need to discuss the rustler incident and the Fourth of July plans."

"Right." Elijah eyed his brother. "And I'm sure Faith doesn't play a part in your trip."

Joshua's cheeks reddened. "Now, Eli, you know it's not like that. Faith—Miss Goodell, I mean—she's just... we're just..."

Elijah clasped his brother on the shoulder. "Go on. Don't keep the lady waiting."

As Joshua rode off toward Mystic, Elijah found his gaze drifting back to Molly. She was sitting next to Little Joe, her hand on the boy's shoulder. Something stirred in Elijah's chest, a feeling he couldn't quite define. It stayed with him the rest of the day and into supper, where he stared across the table to watch her.

After lunch, Elijah walked alongside Molly as the sun rose high above the western mountains. Taking a path around the corrals, their hands brushed together, and for an instant, he almost laced his fingers with hers.

"I never thought I'd say this," Elijah admitted, breaking the silence. "I'm starting to understand why you're so keen on capturing these boys' stories."

"Oh? And what brought about this change of

heart?"

He shrugged, his gaze fixed on the distant mountains. "Seeing you with them. You've got a way of seeing past the surface, I suppose. And you listen well. Sometimes, the boys just need someone to hear them out. You get them to feel good about themselves."

"That's the heart of photography. It's not only about what you see but what you feel. How the subject feels."

They walked on, the silence between them comfortable. As they continued around the barn, Elijah spoke again. "What made you want to become a photographer?"

Her pace slowed, her expression thoughtful. "I've always been fascinated by stories. Everyone has tales to tell and tales they keep hidden. Photography somehow peels away the layers. It's a way to preserve special moments, truths that might otherwise be lost."

He nodded, surprising himself with his genuine interest. "And your family? They support this unconventional path?"

A shadow passed over Molly's face. "Not entirely. My sisters have more traditional aspirations. And my parents..." She trailed off, then squared her shoulders. "But this is my dream, and I intend to see it through."

As they turned back toward the ranch house, Elijah found himself seeing Miss Molly O'Sullivan in a new light. Her determination and passion were qualities he couldn't help admiring, even if he'd never admit it aloud.

Joshua pushed open the door to the Mystic Gazette office, the scent of paper and ink filling his nostrils. His heart quickened at the sight of Faith Goodell, bent over her desk, golden hair twisted into a braid and falling down her back to her waist.

"Evening, Faith," Joshua said, tipping his hat.

She looked up, her stomach fluttering as a smile spread across her face. "Joshua. What a pleasant surprise. I'm finishing up an article on the opening of the apothecary."

"I heard about it. I have another story you might consider printing." Placing his hat on a table, he pulled a chair closer to the desk where she worked.

"So, tell me your idea."

"Rustlers hit us and Tripp Lassiter's ranch. Took about fifty head from each of us and rode to Flatrock."

"In Black Canyon?"

He nodded. "Eli, Nathan, and I rode with Tripp and two of his men. We found the cattle holed up in a pasture surrounded by cliffs not far from Flatrock. They had guards posted. Tripp drew their attention while the rest of us drove off the herd."

"Do you think the rustlers will return?"

Shrugging, he shifted closer to rest his arms on

her desk. "I'd bet on it."

Faith pursed her lips, nodding. "It's a great story. I have enough space to put it right on the first page."

"It's important the town and other ranchers know about the threat to them and their cattle."

"Give me a minute to review my notes."

As she wrote, his gaze wandered over her, as drawn to her now as when they'd sat next to each other in the schoolhouse. He'd known her forever, yet still got a thrill when he saw her.

"So, about a hundred head of cattle?"

"Yep."

"Any idea how many rustlers?"

"We don't know. My guess is about a dozen."

"All right. I have what I need. Thanks for riding into town to tell me what happened." She looked away for a moment before looking back at him. "It's good to see you, Josh."

Standing, he leaned his hip against her desk. "I should've ridden in sooner. The truth is, I was hoping we might discuss the upcoming Fourth of July celebration. I thought perhaps—"

The office door swung open, cutting off Joshua's words. Attorney Braxton Reed strode in, his crisp suit a stark contrast to Joshua's dusty ranch wear.

"Faith," Braxton said, barely acknowledging Joshua's presence. "I've finalized our plans for the Fourth. I've reserved the best seats for the fireworks display. And I put our names in for a table where we can eat. I hate tossing out blankets and sitting on the ground."

Joshua's stomach dropped, his invitation dying on his lips. Faith's eyes darted between the two men, a flicker of something—regret, perhaps—crossing her features.

"That's wonderful, Braxton," she said, her voice lacking its usual enthusiasm. She turned to Joshua, her expression apologetic. "Josh. I'm sorry, you were saying?"

He straightened, forcing a polite smile. "It's nothing important, Faith. I should be getting back to the ranch. Good evening to you both."

As Joshua stepped out into the cooling evening air, he couldn't shake the weight of disappointment settling in his chest. He mounted his horse, casting one last glance at the newspaper office before turning toward home.

Molly O'Sullivan stood on the porch of Wild Spirit Ranch not long after sunup. Her camera and equipment were already packed and loaded onto the buggy, along with her personal belongings. She gazed out at the sprawling landscape, committing every detail to memory.

"It's time," Elijah's gruff voice came from behind her.

She turned, her eyes meeting his. "I suppose it is," she said softly, a hint of regret in her tone. "I can't thank you enough, Elijah. Your help has been invaluable."

He shifted, unused to praise. "I'm glad you came. Glad you spoke with the boys," he muttered.

As they walked toward the barn where the boys were gathered, Molly's mind filled with memories of her time at the ranch. She'd come seeking a story and found so much more.

"Boys," Elijah called out, his voice carrying across the yard. "Miss O'Sullivan is ready to leave."

The young ranch hands gathered around, their faces a mix of emotions. Molly felt a lump form in her throat as she looked at each of them in turn.

"I want you all to know how grateful I am," she began, her voice wavering. "Your stories, your strength, touched me more than I can say."

Gavin stepped forward. "Will you come back, Miss Molly?"

"I hope so, Gavin. When I do, I'll bring the photographs for all of you."

Looking away, she caught Elijah watching her, an unreadable expression on his face. For a moment, their eyes locked, and Molly felt a flutter in her chest.

"Your horse is saddled, Eli," Little Joe said, swiping a tear away.

"Thought I'd ride with you to the boundary." His voice was gruff, but his eyes were softer than usual.

As they set off, a comfortable silence settled between them. The rhythmic clop of hooves and creak of the buggy's wheels filled the air.

After a while, Molly spoke. "I never thought I'd say this, Elijah, but I'm going to miss this place."

His lips twitched in what might have been a smile. "The ranch will miss you, too, Miss Molly O'Sullivan."

They reached the northern boundary, marked by an old, gnarled oak tree. Molly pulled the buggy to a stop, her heart heavy.

"Well," Elijah said, dismounting. "This is where we part ways."

Molly climbed down from the buggy, standing face to face with the taciturn rancher. "Thank you, Elijah. For everything."

For a moment, it seemed as though Elijah might say something more. Instead, he nodded, his gaze intense. "Safe travels, Molly."

Climbing back into the buggy, she slapped the reins. Heading toward Mystic, she couldn't shake the feeling she was leaving a piece of herself behind at Wild Spirit Ranch.

Elijah watched the buggy disappear over the horizon, his expression belying the turmoil within. He turned his horse back toward Wild Spirit Ranch, the vast expanse of Montana stretching before him.

As he rode, Elijah's thoughts drifted to Molly. Her vibrant presence had stirred something in him, something he'd long thought dormant. He shook his head, trying to dispel the thoughts.

"No use dwelling on it," he muttered to himself, urging his horse along the trail.

Chapter Eleven

Molly's buggy rattled along the rutted road to Mystic. She leaned back, letting the warm breeze caress her face. The scent of sage and wheatgrass filled her nostrils, reminding her of the ranch she'd left behind.

"Oh, Elijah," she sighed, gazing at the passing landscape. "I wonder if you'll ever know how much those boys' stories meant to me."

She fingered the leather-bound notebook next to her, filled with interviews and observations from her time at Wild Spirit Ranch. The faces of the boys flashed through her mind, each with a tale of hardship and hope.

As Mystic came into view, Molly straightened her back. She'd been considering the best way to get their stories told. Her contact in Chicago could get her work into neighborhood newspapers. It was unlikely her friend could get the story placed in the Daily Tribune. There was always a chance the business-friendly newspaper would run a story on orphans in Montana as a story their readers might appreciate.

Molly was determined to get the stories published. Then she thought of the local newspaper. As she recalled, it was owned by a woman. Faith something.

"What was her last name," she muttered to herself.

Faith... Faith... Goodell. Yes, Goodell. That was it. The woman Joshua mentioned, and who Elijah said was important to his brother. That would be her first stop. Perhaps Faith would have suggestions for publishing the stories to the world beyond Montana.

Elijah dismounted near the barn. He was greeted by his younger brother, Joshua, who eyed him curiously.

"Everything all right, Eli?" He noted his brother's pensive expression.

Elijah grunted, leading his horse into the barn. "Fine. Just saw Molly off."

Joshua followed him inside, a knowing smile playing on his lips. "Ah, I see. And how'd that go?"

He shot his brother a warning glance. "It went. She's gone. That's all there is to it."

"If you say so," Joshua replied, unconvinced. "You know, Eli, it wouldn't kill you to admit you might miss her."

Elijah busied himself with removing his horse's tack, his movements more forceful than necessary. "What's there to miss? She was here to do a job, and now it's done."

"Whatever you say, brother. I'm not the only one who saw the way you looked at her. It's okay to feel something, you know."

As Joshua walked away, Elijah paused, his hand resting on his horse's flank. He allowed himself a moment of vulnerability, closing his eyes and remembering Molly's smile, her kindness toward the boys.

"Dadgummit," he muttered, his voice barely above a whisper. "Maybe I do miss her."

He shook off the moment of weakness and finished tending to his horse. Leaving the barn, he spotted Grayson by the corral, deep in conversation with a stranger on horseback.

Curiosity piqued, Elijah strode over. As he drew closer, he caught snippets of their hushed conversation.

"...rustlers spotted south of here," the stranger was saying, his voice low and urgent. "I'm afraid they're planning to raid another ranch."

Grayson's face was grim. "Appreciate the warning, Tom. We'll keep an eye out."

Elijah approached, and both men turned to acknowledge him. "What's this about rustlers?" he asked, his eyes narrowing.

Grayson exchanged a glance with the stranger before answering. "Tom here's been hearing rumors. Seems our cattle troubles might not be over."

Elijah blew out a breath. "Just what we need."

Tom shifted in his saddle. "There's more," he said,

his voice tinged with worry. "Word is, they're not just after cattle this time. They're looking for something more."

Elijah's jaw clenched. "What do you mean?"

Tom looked around nervously before leaning in closer. "The man I talked with said they're planning to hit the town during the Fourth of July celebrations. Figured with everyone distracted, the bank could be an easy target."

Grayson shook his head. "We can't let that happen."

Elijah nodded, his mind already considering what they could do. "We'll need to warn the town. Get everyone prepared."

As Tom rode off, Grayson turned to Elijah. "Round up the boys. We've got work to do."

Elijah nodded, his earlier melancholy forgotten in the face of this new threat. As he headed toward the bunkhouse, a chill ran down his spine.

He strode toward the largest corral, where his other brothers and Annalee were breaking horses. His mind churning with ways to combat the ominous news. As was their style, the Becketts would talk in private about what needed to be done, agreeing on a resolution before talking with the orphans.

"Josh! Annalee!" he called out, his voice carrying across the yard. "Round everyone up, we've got trouble brewing. Meet in the house."

It took several minutes before all the Beckett siblings and their mother took seats around the large dining room table.

"What's going on, Grayson?" Joshua asked, his gaze locking on his oldest brother's grim expression.

"It appears we have trouble coming our way," Grayson answered.

Annalee set her arms on the table, leaning forward. "Trouble? What kind of trouble?"

Elijah ran a hand through his hair, his eyes dark with concern. "Rustlers. But it's worse than before. They're planning something big for the Fourth."

Joshua's eyes widened. "The Fourth? But that's when the whole town will be celebrating."

"Exactly." Elijah nodded. "They're counting on the distraction."

Annalee's face set in determination. "Well, we can't let them get away with it. What are we going to do about it?"

Grayson glanced between his siblings, a hint of pride softening his stern features. "We need to warn the town and set up patrols here at the ranch. We've got to be smart about it. We don't want to spook them into changing their plans. The best outcome would be to round up the outlaws and deliver them to the sheriff."

Joshua nodded thoughtfully. "I can ride into Mystic and have a word with the sheriff."

"Good thinking," Grayson agreed. "Annalee, I want you to help Elijah organize the ranch hands and set up a schedule for patrols. We'll need eyes on every corner of our property while continuing our work."

Annalee nodded while looking at Elijah. "We'll get right on it."

Grayson's expression softened. "You'll need to include everyone in the patrols." He glanced around the table. "We know this land better than anyone. If they try to slip through, we'll spot them."

Annalee relaxed, a smile tugging at her lips. "No one will sneak past any of us."

Parker nodded. "We have to be careful how we assign the orphans. Gavin, Jason, and Ted aren't ready to be on patrol by themselves. Samuel would do fine by himself, and so would Little Joe."

"You're right," Elijah said. "One of us will have to be with the younger ones."

"I'd say we leave Gavin, Jason, and Ted here," Grayson countered. "There will be plenty of work for them at the homestead while others are on patrol."

"I agree," Elijah said with a wry grin.

"I want to be included in the patrols." Naomi's announcement surprised them.

"Ma, it would be best for you to stay here with Jolene and the baby," Grayson replied. "I don't want them left alone."

"He's right, Ma," Annalee said. "No telling what would happen if the outlaws show up here when the rest of us are out on patrol."

Naomi grimaced but nodded. "All right. But you all can't be gone at the same time."

"You're right," Grayson said. "Annalee and Elijah will work out the schedules so at least one of us is always here with you." He turned to Joshua. "Ride to Mystic to talk with Brodie. Ask him what more you can do while you're there."

"Such as?" Joshua asked.

"Helping spread the word to business owners and other townsfolk," Grayson said. "They need to be prepared. Brodie and his deputy, Jubal, won't be enough to spread the word."

As Joshua left the house and mounted up, Elijah couldn't shake a nagging worry. He found himself wishing Molly was still at the ranch. But she was long gone, already in Mystic. If what Tom said was accurate, it was the very place the rustlers were targeting.

He shook his head, trying to focus on the task at hand. There was work to be done, and with little information, no time to waste.

Chapter Twelve

The first rays of dawn streaked across the Montana sky, creating a spectacular image of the magnificent mountain range to the east. Elijah Beckett stood on the porch of Wild Spirit Ranch, his calloused hands wrapped around a steaming mug of coffee. As he gazed out at the sprawling expanse of Mystic Valley, his thoughts drifted to Molly O'Sullivan, the feisty photographer who'd captured his attention.

"What are you thinking, big brother?" Annalee's cheerful voice broke through his reverie as she joined him on the porch.

He grunted, taking a sip of his coffee. "About the ride into town."

Her eyes twinkled with mischief. "Thinking about a certain strawberry blonde, more like."

"Annie," he warned.

"Oh, come on, Eli," she teased. "I've seen the way you look at her. It's about time you showed interest in someone."

Sighing, he set down his mug. "We've got more

important things to worry about. We need to find out if Brodie's done anything about the information Josh gave him." He walked down the steps toward the barn. "Come on. We need to get moving."

As they saddled their horses, Elijah found his mind wandering to Molly. Her quick wit and determination had caught him off guard, and he found himself looking forward to seeing her again. It was unfamiliar, both intriguing and unsettling.

The ride into Mystic was filled with Annalee's cheerful chatter, a stark contrast to Elijah's brooding silence. As they approached the town, his keen eyes scanned the surroundings, ever vigilant for any signs of trouble.

"You think there's really going to be trouble during the celebrations?"

Elijah's jaw tightened. "Better to be prepared than caught off guard."

They hitched their horses outside the jail, the mid-morning sun already heating the streets of Mystic. As they entered, Sheriff Brodie Gaines looked up from his desk, his eyes sharp and alert.

"Mornin'," he greeted with a nod, his gaze lingering on Annalee. "What brings you to town?"

Elijah leaned against the wall, arms crossed. "Have you heard anything, Brodie?"

The sheriff's face grew grim. "The information Josh provided seems to be right. Word around town is a gang might be planning to hit the bank during the Fourth of July celebrations. Guess they figure with all the commotion, it'd be the perfect cover."

"The celebration is just two days away," Annalee said. "How can we stop them?"

"That's what we need to figure out," Brodie replied, his gaze sweeping between the Beckett siblings.

As they delved into plans and strategies, Elijah found his thoughts drifting once again to Molly. He wondered if she'd be at the celebrations, camera set up, oblivious to the danger lurking around her. The urge to protect her surged through him, surprising in its intensity.

"Eli?" Annalee's voice cut through his thoughts. "You still with us?"

Straightening, he pushed thoughts of Molly aside. "Yeah, I'm here. Let's figure this out."

Brodie leaned back in his chair, his weathered hands resting on the desk. "I've taken some precautions. Deputized a handful of trustworthy townsfolk. Each one knows how to handle a gun and is willing to stop anyone who attempts to rob the bank. They'll be keeping their eyes peeled during the celebrations."

Elijah nodded, his jaw set. "Smart move. Who'd you pick?"

"Doyle Shaw, Casper Jennings, Josiah Jarvis, Farley Byrne, and Doctor Caleb Wainwright," Brodie replied. "Folks who can handle themselves if things go south."

"Doc Wainwright?" Elijah shook his head. "I never figured him for someone who'd fight."

"He was an Army doctor, posted out here in Indian country before he got out. He's seen his fair share of fighting," Brodie said.

Annalee leaned forward, her eyes bright with determination. "What about me, Brodie? I'm as good a shot as any of them."

Brodie's gaze softened as he looked at her. "Annie, I know you're capable, but—"

"But nothing," she interrupted, her voice firm. "I won't sit idly by while our town's in danger."

Elijah watched the exchange, a mixture of pride and concern for his sister warring within him. He knew Annalee was tough as nails, but the thought of her in harm's way made his stomach churn.

"She's right, Brodie," Elijah found himself saying. "We need capable people we can trust for this."

Brodie sighed, running a hand through his thick hair. "All right, Annalee. You're in. But you stick close to me or Elijah, you hear?"

She beamed. "You got it... Sheriff."

As the meeting wrapped up, Elijah's thoughts once again drifted to Molly. He needed to see her, to make sure she was aware of the potential danger.

"I've got some business to attend to," Elijah announced abruptly. "How about I meet you both at the Golden Griddle in a bit?"

"Fine with me," she answered.

Brodie and Annalee exchanged a knowing look, but Elijah pretended not to notice as he strode out of the sheriff's office.

His boots pounded on the boardwalk as he made his way toward the Mystic Hotel. Elijah barely noticed the intense heat, his mind focused solely on Molly.

As he entered the hotel lobby, the cool air was a welcome relief. The clerk behind the desk looked up, surprise evident on his face at the sight of the taciturn rancher.

"Mr. Beckett," he greeted. "What can I do for you?"

Elijah cleared his throat, suddenly feeling out of place. "I'm here to see Miss O'Sullivan. Is she available?"

The clerk's eyebrows rose, but he nodded. "I'll send someone to fetch her. Please have a seat."

He paced instead, his nerves jangling. What was he doing here? He'd never been one for social calls, yet here he was, seeking out a woman he wasn't sure he liked.

The sound of footsteps on the stairs made him turn. Molly appeared, her eyes widening in surprise as she spotted him.

"Elijah?" she said, a smile spreading across her face. "What a pleasant surprise!"

His heart quickened at the sight of her smile. "Molly," he greeted with a slight nod. "I was hoping you might join me for a walk. There's something important I need to discuss with you."

Her eyebrows arched with curiosity. "Of course," she replied, her voice tinged with both excitement and concern.

As they stepped out onto the bustling street, Elijah felt an unfamiliar nervousness creep over him. He was used to handling ornery cattle and stubborn horses, not escorting beautiful women through town.

He cleared his throat, searching for the right words.

"What have you been doing since you left the ranch?"

She smiled. "Taking as many photographs as possible. Have you been ranching?"

Elijah felt heat rise to his cheeks at her teasing tone. "Suppose I have." He led them toward a quieter side street, away from prying eyes and ears.

"Molly. What I have to tell you is... well, it's not exactly pleasant news."

Her smile faded, replaced by a look of concern. "What is it, Elijah?"

He took a deep breath, steeling himself. "There's a potential threat to the town during the upcoming July Fourth celebrations. Sheriff Gaines has deputized several townsfolk to help keep an eye out, but..." He paused, meeting her gaze directly. "I'd like to offer my services as your personal escort during the festivities. To ensure your safety."

A mix of emotions flashed across her pretty face. Surprise, worry, and something else Elijah couldn't quite place.

"A threat?" she asked, her voice barely above a whisper. "What kind of threat?"

Elijah took a few minutes to explain.

Molly bit down on her lower lip as she processed the information. After a moment, her expression softened, and a mischievous glint appeared in her eyes.

"Well, Mr. Beckett," she said, her tone lighter. "I suppose I'll have to accept your offer of protection.

But I hope you know what you're getting yourself into."

He raised an eyebrow, curiosity piqued. "What do you mean?"

Her lips curved into a playful smile. "I plan to photograph the entire celebration. Every person in the parade, every speech, every firework. And someone will need to carry my equipment box."

A hint of amusement flickered across placid features. "I reckon I can manage that."

They continued their stroll, the tension from earlier dissipating as they fell into a companionable silence. He found himself sneaking glances at Molly, admiring the way the sunlight caught her golden hair.

As they rounded a corner, the inviting facade of the Golden Griddle came into view. The aroma of fresh-baked pies wafted through the air, making Elijah's stomach rumble.

"Elijah! Miss O'Sullivan!" a familiar voice called out.

They turned to see Sheriff Brodie Gaines waving at them from the entrance of the diner. Beside him stood Annalee, her eyes full of curiosity as she took in the sight of her brother with the town's new photographer.

"Why don't you two join us?" Brodie invited, gesturing toward the table. "I hear the sisters just pulled a fresh batch of apple pies from the oven."

Elijah hesitated, glancing at Molly. He found himself reluctant to end their time alone together, but he didn't want to appear rude to his sister and the sheriff.

Elijah cleared his throat, his gaze meeting Brodie's for a brief moment. "Much obliged, but Molly and I will take our own table." His voice was steady, an undercurrent of determination coming through.

Molly's eyebrows rose, a smile playing at the corners of her mouth. She nodded her agreement, and Elijah guided her to an empty table with a light touch on her elbow.

They settled into chairs, the scent of cinnamon and coffee enveloping them. A waitress appeared, setting down two steaming mugs and promising to return with a slice of fresh apple pie for each of them.

She wrapped her hands around her mug, studying Elijah over the rim. "So, tell me about growing up on Wild Spirit Ranch. It must have been quite an adventure."

He took a sip of his coffee, considering her question. He wasn't used to talking about himself, especially not to a woman as intriguing as Molly O'Sullivan. Something in her gaze made him want to open up.

"From the time I was little, Ma and Pa taught us ranch life was hard, honest work. Pa made sure we all learned every task on the ranch, from mending fences to breaking horses."

Molly waited as slices of apple pie were set before them. "I've seen what you do, which is quite demanding. What is your favorite part?"

A rare smile tugged at Elijah's lips. "Rounding up wild mustangs," he admitted. "Nothing's better than thundering across the open range at dawn in pursuit of a wild herd with the whole world spread out before you."

As he spoke, Elijah found himself transported back to those early mornings, the crisp air filling his lungs, the rhythmic pounding of hooves beneath him. He hadn't realized how much he treasured those memories until now, sharing them with Molly.

His reminiscence was interrupted by Molly's next question. "What about your brothers? Did they all take to ranch life as naturally as you?"

He paused, his eyes flickering with a mix of pride and something deeper, more complex. "Not all of us," he said, his voice taking on a thoughtful tone. "My oldest brother, Grayson, had different ambitions for a while."

Molly tilted her head, intrigued. "Oh? What did he do?"

"Grayson became a U.S. Marshal." A hint of admiration crept into his voice. "Wore the badge for a few years, chasing outlaws and keeping the peace. A couple years ago, the ranch called him back. He quit the Marshal service and returned to Wild Spirit with his new bride, Jolene."

As he spoke, Elijah found himself pondering the choices his brothers had made and the paths their lives had taken. His thoughts turned to Cody, and a shadow passed over his face.

Molly, perceptive as ever, noticed the change in his behavior. "And your other brothers?"

His jaw tightened almost imperceptibly. "You've

met all of them, except Cody. He's the next oldest. He left the ranch, too, but for different reasons than Grayson." He wrestled with how much to reveal. Finally, he continued, his voice tinged with sorrow. "Cody's wife and little girl were murdered. After that, he couldn't stay. Became a bounty hunter, chasing the men responsible."

The weight of his words hung heavy between them. Her hand instinctively moved across the table, barely touching Elijah's. "I'm so sorry," she whispered. "Nathan mentioned Cody to me, but didn't provide any details. He was asked to deliver a letter to your mother. He said it was from Cody."

Elijah's impassive face betrayed a flicker of surprise. "A letter? From Cody? I wasn't aware he'd been in contact with anyone in the family. Did you see what it said?"

"No. Nathan didn't open it. At least, not in front of me. I assumed he gave it to your mother."

He chewed a bite of pie, his thoughts on the letter. What could have prompted Cody to write after so long? Was he in trouble? Had he found the men responsible for his family's murder?

Chapter Thirteen

Elijah stood abruptly, then caught himself, remembering his manners. "I'm sorry, Molly. I don't mean to cut our time short, but... I need to ask Ma about the letter."

She waved off his apology with a smile. "I understand. Family comes first."

Before leaving the Golden Griddle, he stopped at his sister's table, whispering in her ear. Annalee glanced across the table at Brodie before nodding.

Outside, they walked toward the Mystic Hotel. Elijah found himself sharing his worries about Cody with Molly.

"He's been out there alone for so long." His voice sounded rougher than usual. "Chasing ghosts and living with his anger. I just hope..." He trailed off, unable to finish the thought.

Molly, sensing his distress, did something that surprised them both. She reached out and took his hand, giving it a gentle squeeze.

Elijah looked down at their joined hands, feeling a

warmth spread through him. For a moment, the worry about Cody faded, replaced by a connection he hadn't expected to feel with this city girl who'd stumbled into his life.

As they approached the hotel, Elijah realized he didn't want to let go. As much as he felt the pull to stay longer, he had to get back to the ranch and talk to his mother about Cody's letter. With reluctance, he released her hand.

"Thank you," he said simply.

Molly smiled, a faint blush coloring her cheeks. "Anytime, Elijah. I hope you're able to learn more about your brother."

Elijah paused at the entrance of the hotel. He turned to Molly, his eyes softening as he gazed at her.

"I appreciate your company today." He touched the brim of his hat, his voice low and sincere. "It was... unexpected, but mighty welcome."

Molly's lips curved into a smile. "I enjoyed it, too. More than I thought I would, truth be told."

A ghost of a smile flitted across Elijah's stony features. As he walked away, his mind was a whirlwind of thoughts about Cody, the letter, and unexpectedly, about the feel of Molly O'Sullivan's hand in his own.

As Elijah rode back to Wild Spirit Ranch with Annalee, the rhythmic clip-clop of their horses' hooves provided a steady backdrop to his swirling thoughts. The vast expanse of Mystic Valley stretched out before them, but Elijah didn't notice the familiar beauty.

"You're awfully quiet, Eli," Annalee remarked, breaking the silence. "More so than usual, I mean."

He grunted, shifting in his saddle. "Just thinking." It wasn't only Cody occupying his thoughts. An image of Molly, her eyes sparkling with laughter, kept pushing its way to the forefront of his mind.

"And?" Annalee pressed, sensing there was more.

"Did you know Ma got a letter from Cody?"

"What? No. She never said anything to me."

"Molly told me Nathan was given a letter to deliver to Ma. Nathan told Molly it was from Cody."

She shook her head. "That can't be right. Ma would've told us."

"Unless Cody asked her not to."

Digesting this, they rode on for several minutes before Annalee questioned him again. "What else is weighing on your mind?"

Elijah sighed, knowing his sister wouldn't let up. "Miss O'Sullivan."

Her eyebrows shot up, surprised he'd admit his fascination for the photographer from Chicago. "I thought you couldn't stand her."

"So did I," he muttered, more to himself than to Annalee. He fell silent again, pondering why this city girl had gotten under his skin. She was everything he tried to avoid. Talkative, stubborn, and far too independent for his liking. And yet he couldn't shove her from his mind.

"There's something about her," he found himself saying. "Can't quite put my finger on it."

Annalee smiled. "Never thought I'd see the day when Elijah Beckett was captivated by a woman."

Elijah scowled at his sister, but there was no real heat behind it. "Don't get ahead of yourself."

As they approached the ranch, he couldn't shake the feeling his future had shifted. Whether it was the mysterious letter from Cody or his unexpected connection with Molly, Elijah sensed change was coming to Mystic Valley. And for once, the prospect didn't displease him.

As they rode past the familiar boulders indicating the entrance to Wild Spirit Ranch, the familiar scent of sage and horses filled the air. The evening light painted shadows across the weathered buildings and corrals of their homestead.

As they approached the house, she broke the silence. "You gonna ask Ma about Cody's letter?"

His jaw tightened. "I've been thinking about it. Reckon I will."

They dismounted, and as he led his horse to the barn, he spotted a familiar figure emerging from the house. Naomi Beckett, her brown hair streaked with gray, strode toward them.

"There you are," she called out, her voice carrying a hint of worry. "I was beginning to wonder if you'd decided to move to town permanently."

Elijah couldn't help smiling. "No chance of that, Ma. We had some business to attend to."

Naomi's keen eyes studied her son's face. "And

did this business have anything to do with that photographer from Chicago?"

Annalee snickered, earning a sharp look from Elijah. He turned back to his mother. "Partly. There's something else we need to discuss."

Naomi's expression grew serious. "What is it?"

He took a deep breath. "It's about Cody. I understand he sent you a letter."

She stared at him, not showing a trace of guilt. "You heard right."

"Were you planning to share the news with the rest of the family?"

"I hadn't decided."

The knot in Elijah's stomach tightened. "Ma... don't you think we'd like to know where he is, if he's safe, and if he's coming home?"

"I can tell you he's safe. Cody also located the men who killed Miriam and Sophia."

Annalee stepped closer. "Did he kill them?"

"He didn't say."

"What about coming home?" Annalee persisted.

Naomi sighed. "The letter wasn't clear. He knows how much we want him to return. The boy has to decide for himself."

As they walked up the steps to the house, a distant rumble of thunder echoed across the valley. Elijah glanced at the darkening sky, a chill running down his spine. Whatever storm was brewing, he had a sinking feeling it was about more than the weather.

Molly stood at the edge of Mystic at sunrise, her camera forgotten as she gazed out at the vast expanse of the Montana frontier. She'd pulled her strawberry blonde hair into a braid, yet the wind whipped errant strands across her face. Brushing them away, she inhaled the pleasant scent of prairie grass mixed with sage.

She'd planned this for the last week. Her idea was to take pictures of July Fourth, starting with the sunrise and ending with the fireworks. Looking out at the endless horizon, her doubts returned.

"What am I doing here?" she whispered to herself, her voice barely audible over the rustling grass. The question had been gnawing at her for days, growing louder with each passing moment. She'd left behind the comforts of Chicago, the security of her family's home, and the familiarity of city life. For what? A dream of adventure? The allure of the unknown?

Molly set her hand on the stand holding her camera, the familiar wood frame a stark reminder of her purpose. Yet, as she looked out at the untamed wilderness before her, doubt crept in like a shadow.

"I don't belong here," she muttered, her words tinged with a mix of frustration and longing. "This isn't my world. I'm not cut out for this life."

Images of Chicago's bustling streets and elegant parties flashed through her mind, a stark contrast to the rugged simplicity of Mystic. She could almost hear her mother's voice gently chiding her for this foolish adventure.

"Maybe I should go back," Molly said, her voice wavering. "Back to civilization, back to where I understand the rules."

But even as the words left her lips, something inside her rebelled against the idea. She thought of the photographs she'd taken, the raw beauty she'd captured through her lens. The frontier had a wildness, a freedom that both terrified and exhilarated her.

Her thoughts drifted to Elijah Beckett, and her heart quickened. His forceful presence and quiet strength had drawn her in, despite her best efforts to maintain her independence.

"Oh, Elijah," she sighed. "Why do you have to complicate things?"

The mere thought of him sent a shiver down her spine, a confusing blend of attraction and apprehension. Molly closed her eyes, trying to sort through the tangle of emotions.

"I can't let myself fall for him," she said firmly, as if speaking the words aloud would make them true. "I came here to be independent, to make my own way. Not to... not to..."

She couldn't bring herself to finish the thought. The idea of a relationship with Elijah thrilled her one moment and terrified her the next. He represented everything she'd learned about this new world. Rugged, unpredictable, drawing her in with intense passion.

"But what if I'm not strong enough for this life? What if I'm not cut out to be a frontier woman?"

The sun rose over the horizon, signaling the time had come to pack away her camera and make her way back to the hotel. Elijah would be arriving soon, and she wanted to be ready.

Molly stood there, caught between two worlds, her heart torn between the familiar comforts of her past and the wild promise of her future. The Montana wind swirled around her, as if urging her to make a choice, to embrace the unknown or retreat to safety.

Molly O'Sullivan stood on the precipice of decision, her life balanced on the edge of a new frontier.

Her fingers tightened into fists at her sides. She took a deep breath, the crisp Montana air filling her lungs and steeling her resolve.

"No," she said aloud, her voice firm. "I didn't come all this way to turn back now."

With renewed determination, Molly returned to the hotel, carrying her camera box with both hands. She stopped at the front desk and asked to see their map of the Pacific Northwest. Her eyes traced the route of the railroad to Seattle, her mind already composing the shots she'd capture along the way. The rugged Cascades and the misty shores of Puget Sound. Each image would be a testament to her growth and bravery.

I'll prove I belong out here, she thought, plotting her journey. *To everyone else and to myself.*

Satisfied, she lugged her camera upstairs to her room. Changing her clothes, she redid her braid. A knock at her door startled her from her planning. She opened it to find Elijah Beckett, his tall frame filling the doorway.

"Molly," he said, his voice clipped but not unkind. "The celebrations are starting soon."

Her heart skipped. "I'm ready. Thank you for offering to escort me today."

Elijah picked up her camera case, motioning for her to precede him down the stairs. As they walked toward Mystic's main square, Molly found herself stealing glances at Elijah. His strong profile was illuminated by the rising sun, and she itched to capture it on film.

"You seem different today," Elijah observed, breaking the silence.

She smiled. "I've made some decisions. About my future."

Elijah raised an eyebrow. "Oh?"

"I'm continuing on to Seattle after I photograph Yellowstone," she explained, her voice gaining confidence with each word. "This journey is important to me. I need to see it through."

"It's an admirable goal. Takes guts to forge your own path. Especially out here, where danger is always close by."

As they neared the festivities, the air filled with laughter and music. Molly felt a warmth spread through her chest, realizing she was genuinely looking forward to celebrating with these people. And with Elijah.

"Thank you," she said softly. "For understanding."

Elijah's hand brushed hers, sending a jolt through her. "Reckon we're not so different, you and I," he murmured. "Both of us trying to carve out our place in this wild country."

Their eyes met, and for a moment, the noise of the celebration faded away. In their shared glance, she saw a glimpse of a future she hadn't dared to imagine. Perhaps a future where her independence and her growing feelings for Elijah might coexist.

Chapter Fourteen

They weaved through the crowd, the festive atmosphere of Mystic's Fourth of July celebrations enveloping them. Colorful bunting adorned storefronts, and the scent of roasted corn and barbecue filled the air. Children darted about, their laughter mingling with the twang of a nearby fiddle.

"I never thought I'd see anything like this out here," Molly remarked, her eyes wide with wonder. "It's almost as if I'm back in Chicago. Only, this is better."

Elijah's lips tipped upward. "Reckon we know how to celebrate out here. Though I'd wager our corn tastes better than anything you city folk can rustle up."

Molly laughed, a warm, genuine sound making Elijah's heart skip a beat. "Is that a challenge? Because I'll have you know, I make a decent corn chowder."

"That so?" His eyes sparkled with amusement. "Might have to try it for myself sometime."

As they strolled, she found herself surprised by how easily the conversation flowed between them. Elijah seemed to open up in her presence. They discussed everything from her dry plate photography to the challenges of ranch life.

"I never realized how much work goes into running a ranch," Molly admitted. "What your family has built is quite impressive."

He nodded, a hint of pride in his voice. "There's something about working the land, being part of something bigger than yourself. It's worth the long days and hard work."

She felt a pang of longing. "I can see why you love it so much. It must be nice, having such deep roots."

Before Elijah could respond, Sheriff Brodie Gaines approached, his customary serious expression softened by the day's festivities.

"Elijah, Miss O'Sullivan," he greeted them with a nod. "Enjoying the celebration?"

"It's wonderful, Sheriff," Molly replied. "Though I hope you're allowing yourself some fun as well?"

His lips twitched. "Keeping watch on the townsfolk, ma'am. Can't be too careful."

Elijah exchanged a meaningful look with Brodie. "Any sign of trouble?"

He shook his head. "Nothing. Our precautions may have scared them off. Those outlaws would be foolish to try anything today."

Molly glanced between them, sensing the undercurrent of tension. Elijah had already told her about the possible threat. "What do you think will happen?"

Elijah placed a reassuring hand on her arm. "We aren't certain anything will happen, Molly. Could be the talk about the outlaws robbing the bank today was a rumor."

Brodie nodded in agreement. "We've got extra men patrolling, and the bank's locked up tight. Everyone is safe."

As the sheriff moved on, Molly couldn't shake a nagging feeling of unease. She studied Elijah's face, noting the slight furrow in his brow. "You're sure everything's all right?"

His expression softened as he met her gaze. "You're safe here with me. Now, how about we go see about getting some food before the fireworks start?"

As they made their way to the food tables, Molly pushed her concerns aside, determined to enjoy this unexpected day of joy and connection.

As Lorna Dunne, owner of the Buffalo Run Tavern, handed her a plate of carved beef and carrot salad, the crack of gunfire shattered the festive atmosphere. Molly's heart leapt into her throat as screams erupted from the direction of the bank.

"Get down!" Elijah's voice cut through the chaos, his strong hands pushing her toward the ground, the plate of food slipping from her hands.

Fear gripped her as she crouched behind a wooden crate. Her hand instinctively reached for her camera. Then she remembered Elijah had set it behind the table.

"What's happening?" she gasped.

Elijah's face was a mask of grim determination.

"The bank. It's a robbery." His gaze met hers, fierce and protective. "Stay here. Don't move."

"But I can help!" Molly protested, crawling around the table toward her camera. "I can document this, show people what's happening!"

"No. It's too dangerous," Elijah growled, his hand on her shoulder. "Listen to me, Molly. I can't protect you if you're out there."

The sounds of panic swelled around them. Shattering glass, thundering hoofbeats, screams, and gunshots underscored his concern. Molly's heart pounded, torn between her instinct to capture this moment of history and her fear of the very real danger.

"We need to get these people to safety." Elijah's gaze scanned the crowd as more gunshots sounded. He turned to a group huddled nearby. "You there! Head for the church, it's the sturdiest building in town."

As Elijah directed people, Molly's thoughts whirled. This was the kind of story she'd come west to document. But the fear in people's eyes, the children crying, stopped her from grabbing the camera box. This was more than a thrilling tale for her camera.

"Elijah! What can I do to help?"

He paused, conflict clear on his face. "Help guide people toward the church. Promise me you won't go near the bank."

"I promise. Be careful, Elijah."

As he moved off to assist with thwarting the outlaws, Molly took a deep breath. This wasn't Chicago, with its predictable streets and civilized dangers. This was the untamed West she'd dreamed of capturing. Now, faced with its reality, she realized how unprepared she truly was.

Molly crouched low, scanning the chaotic scene. The Fourth of July decorations fluttered in the breeze, mocking them. A stark contrast to the mayhem unfolding.

Spotting a group of three women and several children, she rushed to them. "You need to get to the church. Go between the buildings and follow the others."

"Thank you," one of the women said, her voice trembling.

"Do you need me to go with you?"

"No, we can make it." They turned and hurried away as gunfire sounded again.

Molly turned to see a group of masked men burst from the bank, guns raised and sacks bulging with stolen cash. Their leader, a towering figure with a black bandana covering his face, fired a shot into the air.

"Nobody move!" he bellowed. His voice carried over the panicked screams.

Before he could say anything more, gunfire from the men of Mystic slammed into the outlaw's body. One by one, the other members of the gang fell to the onslaught of bullets.

Molly's heart raced, but her hands remained steady. If only her camera were set up. She'd capture the raw fear on people's faces, the determined set of

Sheriff Brodie's jaw as he ducked behind a water trough, his revolver at the ready. Instead, she'd only see the images in her mind.

"Miss O'Sullivan!"

Molly turned to see Faith Goodell, owner of the Mystic Gazette, crouched behind an overturned table. When the sound of gunfire slowed, she rushed to kneel beside her.

"Are you all right, Miss Goodell?"

Faith's eyes gleamed with a mix of fear and journalistic fervor. "This'll be the story of the year. If I survive to print it."

"I'll take photographs, but they'll show the aftermath."

"That will do," Faith said.

A commotion near the bank drew their attention. One of the robbers had grabbed a young woman, using her as a human shield.

"Let her go!" Elijah's voice rang out, clear and commanding. He, Brodie, and Jubal walked toward him, their guns aimed at his chest. "You'll never make it away from here," Elijah said. "Let her go and put down your gun."

Molly's breath caught in her throat. What was Elijah doing?

The robber let out a nervous laugh, a harsh, grating sound. "I'm going to ride away and take her with me."

Elijah took another step toward him, seeing the stark fear in the young woman's eyes. "There are at least eight guns aimed at you. You'll never make it to your horse."

Molly's breath caught. She had to do something, anything to help.

As if sensing her thoughts, Faith grabbed Molly's arm. "Don't even think about it," she whispered. "We document. That's how we help."

Molly blew out a breath, her jaw set. She might not be able to fight, but she could bear witness with her camera.

Elijah's eyes darted to Molly, a flicker of concern thawing his stony features. In that instant, he seemed to make a decision. With deliberate slowness, he began to edge toward her, his body angled to shield her from potential gunfire.

"Let the woman go," Brodie yelled at the outlaw. "You'll get a fair trial. Right now, the charge is attempted robbery. Don't make it worse."

The outlaw seemed to consider his chance of getting away against facing a jury. "All right." Letting go of the woman, he dropped his gun, raising his hands in the air.

With the danger gone, Molly rushed to set up her camera. Positioning it toward the bank, she took a photograph of Brodie marching the man toward her on the way to the jail. Changing plates, she took another photograph.

Her fingers tightened on the camera, positioning it to focus on Elijah. He stared straight back at her. *The perfect image*, she thought before capturing him in a picture Molly knew would be shown across the country.

Chapter Fifteen

The acrid smell of gunpowder lingered in the air as Elijah Beckett stood motionless, his eyes fixed on the undertaker's wagon. Calum Post, the town's somber-faced mortician, methodically loaded the bodies of the fallen outlaws, each thud of lifeless flesh against wood sending a shiver down Elijah's spine. His hands, normally steady as iron, trembled with relief and gnawing concern for Molly's safety.

Elijah clenched his fists, willing the tremors to subside. "Pull yourself together," he muttered under his breath, his jaw tightening as he surveyed the chaotic aftermath of the shootout. His gaze darted around, searching for a glimpse of strawberry blonde hair amidst the crowd.

Finally, he spotted her. Molly O'Sullivan stood near the boardwalk, her camera box beside her, eyes wide with shock. Without hesitation, Elijah strode toward her, his long legs eating up the distance between them.

"Molly," he called out, his hard-edged features

cracking as relief flooded his voice.

"Elijah, I—"

Before she could finish, Elijah pulled her into a fierce embrace, his strong arms enveloping her smaller frame. He buried his face in her hair, inhaling the faint scent of lavender mixed with sage that always clung to her, grounding himself in the reality she was safe.

"Are you all right?" Pulling back, he examined her face, his gaze searching hers.

She nodded, her chin lifting with characteristic determination. "I'm fine, Elijah. It takes more than a few bullets flying to rattle me."

A ghost of a smile tugged at the corners of his mouth. "Stubborn as ever, I see."

"Would you rather me be dull and mousy?" A spark of her usual fire returned to her eyes.

His expression softened, his usual taciturn nature giving way to a moment of vulnerability. "No, I wouldn't," he admitted. "When I heard the shots... I thought..."

She placed a hand on his chest, her touch soothing the rapid beating of his heart. "I'm okay, truly. What about you? Are you hurt?"

Elijah shook his head, his gaze drifting back to the undertaker's wagon. "No, I'm fine. Just... it was too close. Much too close."

"I know," she murmured, following his gaze. "It seems we're both safe."

Elijah nodded, his arm still wrapped around her shoulders. He knew he should let go and maintain the proper distance propriety demanded. For reasons eluding him, he couldn't bring himself to break contact. The warmth of her body against his was a tangible reminder they'd survived, and the danger had passed.

"Your camera." He looked at the box on the boardwalk. "Did you manage to get any pictures?"

Molly's eyes lit up, her passion for her craft overshadowing the gravity of the situation. "A few. Not as many as I would've liked. Still, what I have will be on the front page in every paper from here to Chicago."

He couldn't help chuckling at her enthusiasm, marveling at how fast she bounced back from danger. It was one of the things he admired most about her. Molly possessed an indomitable spirit, refusing to be cowed by the harsh realities of frontier life.

"You're something else, Molly O'Sullivan," he said, shaking his head in fond exasperation. "A good number of women would be swooning or crying after what happened."

She raised an eyebrow, a challenging glint in her eye. "Well, I'm not most women. Besides, someone has to document the truth of life out here. Might as well be me."

Elijah's expression grew serious once more. "Just be careful, all right? I can't always be around to protect you."

"I don't need protecting, Elijah Beckett," Molly retorted, her chin jutting out. "I can take care of myself."

He sighed, knowing better than to argue. "I know

you can. The same as I'm certain there are a few people around here who'd miss you if you got yourself killed."

Their eyes met, an unspoken current passing between them. The moment was broken when the church doors slammed open.

"Look at that," Molly murmured.

Elijah followed her gaze, his tolerant expression softening as he observed a large group of people spilling out from the church's double doors. Men helped women down the steps while children darted between the adults' legs, their laughter a welcome contrast to the recent gunshots.

As they watched, more people began to emerge from various storefronts. The door to Jennings Mercantile creaked open, revealing the round face of Mrs. Jennings, the shopkeeper's wife. She blinked, clutching her shawl around her ample frame before stepping outside. Spotting Elijah, she waved, a broad smile transforming her face.

Before Elijah could respond, a commotion near the center of town drew their attention. Mayor Carl Jurgen had appeared, his thinning brown hair ruffled and his waistcoat slightly askew. Despite his disheveled appearance, the mayor's voice rang out clear and strong.

"Good people of Mystic!" He spread his arms wide in a welcoming gesture. "I assure you, the danger has passed. Our brave sheriff and his deputy have dealt with the miscreants swiftly and decisively."

Elijah and Molly exchanged a look, a mix of

amusement and respect passing between them. The mayor, for all his faults, knew how to command a crowd.

"Furthermore," Jurgen continued, his words tumbling out in his characteristic rushed manner, "I see no reason why this unfortunate incident should derail our plans for celebration. The Fourth of July festivities will proceed as scheduled!"

A murmur of excitement rippled through the gathering crowd. Molly's eyes widened, her earlier tension melting away. "Oh, Elijah, isn't that wonderful? We'll still have the fireworks and everything."

His lips quirked in a half-smile, unable to resist her infectious enthusiasm. "I suppose it is," he admitted. "Though I reckon the real fireworks happened a bit early today."

She laughed, the sound clear and bright in the afternoon air. "Always the cynic, aren't you? Come on, admit it. You're looking forward to the fireworks as much as anyone."

His features softened as he looked at her, marveling at her ability to find joy, even in the aftermath of danger. Elijah's gaze shifted to the heavy camera equipment at Molly's feet.

"We should get your camera to the jail," he said. "I'm certain Brodie will let you take a photograph of the outlaw."

Molly nodded, her earlier excitement tempered by the gravity of the task ahead. "You're right. Afterward, I'll move the camera out here for the puppet show."

Elijah lifted the camera equipment and strode to the jail. As they made their way along the boardwalk, Molly scanned the town for other opportunities to capture with her camera.

"You know," Molly mused. "I never thought I'd be taking pictures of outlaws when I came out west. It's all quite exciting."

Elijah grunted, his expression neutral. "Excitement's overrated, if you ask me. Give me a quiet day on the ranch any time."

They arrived at the jailhouse, where Brodie stood by the window, his tall frame silhouetted against the weathered wooden interior. He nodded at Elijah before shifting his attention to Molly.

"What can I do for you, Miss O'Sullivan?"

Inside the jail, the atmosphere was tense. The captured outlaw sat hunched on his cot, his gaze darting between Molly and her camera.

"Would you allow me to take a photograph with you and the prisoner?"

Shifting, Brodie looked at the man in the cell. "Don't see why not."

As Elijah set up the camera, Molly addressed the prisoner. "Sir, I'm going to take your photograph now. It won't hurt, I assure you."

The outlaw stood and walked to the door of his cell. "Don't make no difference to me, lady. Take your photograph and be done with it."

Molly's jaw tightened, but she maintained her composure. She positioned herself behind the camera, framing the shot with Brodie standing stoically by the cell.

"Hold still, please," she instructed, her voice steady despite the undercurrent of tension in the room.

Molly's heart hammered with nervous energy as she captured the image. Straightening, she smiled to herself. She'd photographed a real outlaw.

"Thank you, Sheriff," Molly announced, already packing up her equipment. "Elijah, could you help me move this to the puppet show? I'd like to photograph the children before the fireworks."

Outside, Molly knelt beside her camera case, her gaze intent as she counted the remaining dry plates. "Four left," she murmured, more to herself than to Elijah. "I hope it's enough for the fireworks."

Elijah leaned against a nearby post, his eyes scanning the bustling street. "Are you able to purchase more at the mercantile?"

"Yes and no. Mr. Jennings ordered more for me. They'll arrive on the next railroad from the East."

She looked up at him. "I've never photographed fireworks before, so I don't know what to expect." Molly set the plates aside and stood, brushing dust from her skirt.

They watched the townsfolk from the edge of the boardwalk outside the jail, their shoulders nearly touching. The street was alive with excitement as families with children, couples, and groups of cowboys sought the best spots for the impending display.

"Look at them all," Molly mused, her gaze sweeping over the crowd. "It's as if the shootout never happened."

Elijah nodded. "Folks here are resilient. Have to be."

Molly turned to study his profile, noticing the tension in his shoulders. "Does it ever get easier? Dealing with all of this?" She gestured to where the shootout took place.

He was quiet for a long moment, his eyes fixed on some distant point. "Life isn't easy, no matter where you live," he finally said. "There are good days, and others not so good."

A group of children raced by, their laughter cutting through the evening air. Molly watched them go, a wistful expression crossing her face. "I wonder what my sisters would think of all this. They always said I was foolish for wanting to come out west."

"And what do you think?" Elijah asked, his gaze now fixed on her.

Molly met his eyes, a spark of defiance igniting within her. "I think they're the foolish ones for never daring to try."

The creak of the jail door drew their attention. Brodie stepped out onto the boardwalk, his keen gaze sweeping over the street before settling on Elijah and Molly.

"Back to normal, I see," he said.

"We were just talking about how quickly the people returned after the danger was over." Molly looked down at her camera nestled safely beside her.

Elijah's gaze flickered between Brodie and the jail.

"How's your guest settling in?"

Brodie's lips twitched in a humorless smile. "About as well as you'd expect. He's not exactly pleased with his accommodations. Jubal's going to keep watch on him for a spell."

"Speaking of unwelcome guests," Elijah said, his voice dropping slightly. "Calum Post is handling the bodies from the shoot-out."

Brodie shifted, his gaze moving to the Golden Griddle. "It'll be good to get this behind us. I appreciate the warning you Becketts gave me."

Elijah gave a slight nod. "Have you seen my sister?"

"Annalee?" Brodie asked.

Chuckling, Elijah shared a look with Molly before facing Brodie. "Who else? I don't believe Lily came into town with everyone else."

Brodie's face flushed enough for Molly to notice. "Truth is, she'll be coming to the jail after your family finishes their meal at the Golden Griddle. Guess I should go talk to Calum about the bodies."

"It's a grim business, but I reckon it's best to have it dealt with quickly," Elijah said. "Less chance of complications."

Molly looked between the two men, her brows drawing together. "Complications?"

The men exchanged a glance, a wealth of unspoken understanding passing between them.

"Sometimes, Miss O'Sullivan, the departed have friends or family who might take issue with how things played out," Brodie answered. "Best to have everything squared away before any such individuals might arrive."

Her eyes widened as the implications sank in. "I see. It's easy to forget there are always two sides to these stories."

Elijah's jaw tightened, his eyes hardening. "Those men made their choice when they rode into town with guns drawn. They knew the risks."

"I'm not arguing that," Molly countered, her voice firm. "But it doesn't make it any less tragic."

Brodie cleared his throat but didn't respond. As he turned to leave, a flicker of movement caught his eye. A familiar figure emerged from the Golden Griddle. Annalee Beckett approached the group, her smile widened when her gaze settled on Brodie.

"Evening, everyone," Annalee said brightly, her gaze lingering on Brodie for a moment before sweeping across the others. "I hope I'm not interrupting anything important."

"Not at all, Annalee," Molly said. "We were just discussing the events of the day."

Elijah glanced at his sister. "Looking forward to the fireworks, Annie?"

Her face lit up with enthusiasm. "Oh, yes. It's not every day we get such excitement in Mystic. Well, aside from today's unexpected drama, of course."

Brodie's posture stiffened at Annalee's casual reference to the shoot-out. "It's been quite a day," he agreed, his tone neutral. "The fireworks should help folks put it behind them."

As the conversation continued, Elijah found himself studying Annalee, wondering how deep his sister's feelings were for Brodie.

Suddenly, a shout pierced the air, followed immediately by a scream from inside the jail. The sound cut through the evening's festive atmosphere like a knife, causing the group to freeze.

Elijah's hand flew to his gun, his eyes locking with Brodie's in a moment of shared alarm. Molly and Annalee both gasped, instinctively drawing closer together on the boardwalk.

"What in tarnation?" Brodie muttered, already turning toward the jail, his hand on his pistol.

The scream came again, louder this time, followed by several gunshots.

The jail door burst open with a thunderous bang, and Deputy Jubal Whitton stumbled out onto the boardwalk. His blond hair was disheveled, a trickle of blood running down his temple. He staggered, nearly falling, before catching himself on the doorframe.

"Sheriff!" Jubal gasped, his eyes wild with panic. "They've broken him out!"

Chapter Sixteen

"The outlaw's partners. They came out of nowhere!" Jubal slumped against the door of the jail. Molly and Annalee rushed to him, stopping when the deputy held up a hand. "I'm fine, ladies. Just a little scratch."

"How many, Jube?" Brodie demanded.

"Three, maybe four," Jubal panted, wiping blood from his eye. "They had the drop on me before I could even draw. I'm sorry, Sheriff. I tried—"

"It's not your fault," Brodie cut him off. He turned to Elijah. "I'm going inside. Watch the ladies."

"We can watch ourselves," Molly shot back at him.

"Fine," Brodie called over his shoulder.

Jubal followed close behind. Elijah looked at Molly, torn between the desire to help Brodie and the need to protect the women.

"Go on with you," Annelee said. Molly nodded, ending Elijah's internal struggle. Drawing his gun, he slipped inside.

Brodie's broad shoulders tensed as he surveyed the damage inside the jail. Moments later, the sheriff emerged, Jubal and Elijah right behind him, his face a mask of frustration and anger. "The window's been torn clean out," he growled, gesturing behind him. "Cell's empty. They're long gone by now."

He looked at his deputy. "Did you see which direction they headed?"

Jubal shook his head. "Down the alley to the south. They could be anywhere by now. Flatrock, maybe. Or Black Canyon."

Annalee stepped closer to Brodie, her voice steady despite the fear in her eyes. "Maybe we need to warn everyone. Cancel the fireworks, get people inside."

"No," Brodie said, surprising them all. "We can't let these outlaws disrupt our lives more than they already have. They're long gone by now. The fireworks go on."

Molly raised an eyebrow. "You sure about that, Sheriff?"

His gaze hardened. "It's exactly what we need to do. Show them we won't be cowed. Besides, it'll keep folks in one place, where we can watch over them." With himself and just one deputy, Brodie knew chasing the gang would leave the town defenseless. He also knew he could no longer put off talking to the mayor about hiring another deputy. "I'll be back soon. There's someone I have to talk to."

Annalee watched him leave, disappointed but knowing Brodie wouldn't have left if it wasn't important.

Jubal, still nursing his head, looked after him. "The sheriff was right. Those outlaws aren't going to come back. At least not today."

The sound of fireworks whistling into the sky made them all look up. It was time to enjoy what was left of the July Fourth celebrations.

The moonlit silhouettes of ponderosa pines were a familiar sight as Elijah Beckett and his siblings rode their horses back to Wild Spirit Ranch. The July Fourth fireworks still echoed in his mind, though Molly O'Sullivan's radiant smile consumed his thoughts. He couldn't shake the image of her emerald eyes sparkling in the glow of the fireworks, her infectious laughter ringing out over the crowd's cheers.

"Quite a show tonight." Annalee's voice cut through Elijah's reverie. Her eyes twinkled with mischief as she nudged her horse closer to his. "I noticed you watching Molly more than the fireworks."

His jaw clenched, his grip tightening on the reins. "No more than I watched anyone else," he muttered, avoiding his sister's knowing gaze.

Joshua chuckled, shaking his head. "Sure you were. And I'm the King of England."

"Leave him be," Nathan interjected, his voice tinged with exhaustion. "We're all too tired to appreciate your teasing."

As they crested the final hill before the ranch,

Elijah's thoughts drifted back to Molly. Her fierce independence and quick wit had caught him off guard, challenging his preconceptions about city women. He found himself yearning to know more about her, to unravel the mystery behind those captivating eyes.

The group dismounted at the barn, their movements sluggish with fatigue. Elijah's muscles ached as he began unsaddling his horse.

"We've got our work cut out for us tomorrow," Joshua said, stifling a yawn. "The new corral won't build itself."

Annalee lifted the saddle off her horse's back, a tired smile playing on her lips. "And don't forget about mending the fence line in the horse pasture. The herd will run right through it if they can."

Elijah nodded, his mind already mapping out the tasks ahead. "Parker and I will take care of the new corral," he offered. "Nate, you and Josh can work on the fence line."

As they finished tending to their horses, Elijah found himself lingering in the barn. The sweet scent of hay and leather surrounded him, a comforting reminder of home. Yet, for the first time in years, he felt a restlessness stirring within him.

"You coming, Elijah?" Joshua called from the doorway.

He shook his head, forcing himself back to the present. "Yeah, I'll be right there."

As he followed his siblings toward the house, Elijah couldn't help but wonder what tomorrow would bring. Would Molly visit the ranch again? The thought sent a thrill of anticipation through him, even as he tried to temper his growing feelings.

As Elijah tried to sleep an hour later, his thoughts were filled with flashes of green eyes and the sound of laughter carried on the Montana wind.

He tossed and turned in his bed, the moonlight streaming through his window. His mind consumed with thoughts of Molly. He squeezed his eyes shut, willing the images away.

"She's leaving," he muttered to himself, his voice barely audible in the quiet room. "She'll be gone soon, and there's nothing you can do about it."

Try as he might, Elijah couldn't shake the warmth in his chest when he thought of her. He sat up, running a hand through his tousled hair. "Control yourself, Beckett," he chided himself. "She's a city girl. This isn't her life."

As the first hints of dawn began to color the sky, Elijah gave up on sleep. He swung his legs over the side of the bed, setting his jaw. There was work to be done, and he refused to let some fleeting feelings get in the way of his responsibilities.

He dressed quickly, his movements quick and efficient. As he made his way down to the kitchen, the floorboards creaked under his boots.

"You're up early," came a voice from the dimly lit

room.

Elijah started, then relaxed as he recognized his mother's silhouette. "Mornin', Ma. Thought I'd get an early start on the day."

Naomi Beckett studied her son, a knowing look in her eyes. "Couldn't sleep?"

Shrugging, he busied himself with pouring a cup of coffee. "Eager to get to work."

His mother's soft chuckle made him turn. "You know, Eli, there's no shame in admitting when something's got you all twisted up inside."

"I don't know what you're talking about."

Naomi sighed, patting his arm as she passed. "Of course not. Well, since you're up, might as well put those restless hands to good use. The biscuits are ready to be rolled out and cut. Then you can put them into the oven."

Working the dough, his thoughts drifted once more to Molly. The image sent a jolt through him, and he rolled the dough with renewed vigor.

I can't think like that. She's leaving. End of story.

Even as he tried to convince himself, a part of him held onto hope. There was always hope Molly might see something worth staying for in Mystic Valley.

Placing the biscuits into the oven, Elijah stepped out onto the porch, his eyes scanning the vast expanse of Wild Spirit Ranch. The day's tasks stretched out before him, a welcome distraction from his tumultuous thoughts.

The sun climbed higher in the sky as Elijah and his siblings threw themselves into the day's work. Sweat glistened on their brows as they dug holes and set the heavy wooden posts for the new corral.

"Eli!" Grayson called out, his deep voice carrying over the sound of hammering. "How's that corner post looking?"

Elijah stepped back, eyeing the sturdy post he'd just set. "It's solid. Should hold up against even the orneriest bull."

Naomi appeared, carrying two canteens. "Speaking of ornery," she teased, "you boys better take a break before you keel over."

As they gulped down water, Elijah's gaze wandered to the distant shimmer of Moon River. "We ought to check on the herd down by the water. Make sure none of those calves have wandered off again."

Grayson nodded, wiping his brow. "Good thinking. Why don't you head down there? Ride the river for a bit. Make sure nothing's blocking the flow. I can finish up here."

Elijah mounted his horse, relishing the familiar creak of leather. As he rode toward the river, the rhythmic pounding of hooves matched the steady beat of his heart. The physical exertion had done wonders to quiet his restless mind.

Hours later, his muscles aching from the day's labor, Elijah guided his mount back toward the ranch house. He felt good about what he'd accomplished.

As he crested the final hill, something caught his eye. There, parked in front of the house, sat a familiar buggy. Elijah's heart leapt into his throat.

"Molly?" he whispered, hardly daring to hope.

Energized, Elijah urged his horse forward. He all but flew into the yard, dismounting with practiced ease. His hands trembled as he untacked his mount.

"Get ahold of yourself," he muttered, taking a deep breath.

But even as he admonished himself, Elijah couldn't help the anticipation building in his chest. He strode toward the house, his long legs eating up the distance. As he reached for the door handle, he paused, steeling himself for whatever awaited him inside.

With one last steadying breath, Elijah pushed open the door. Hearing feminine voices, he stepped into the kitchen, his heart pounding against his ribs.

His breath caught at the sight before him. There, standing at the counter with flour dusting her hands and a stray lock of strawberry blonde hair falling across her forehead, was Molly. She was laughing at something his sister, Lilian, had said, her eyes sparkling with mirth.

The sight of her hit Elijah in the gut. Joy and relief washed over him in equal measure. He stood frozen in the doorway, drinking in the scene before him. Molly appeared so at ease in his family's kitchen, working alongside his mother and sister as if she belonged there.

"Elijah." His mother's voice broke through his reverie. "Look who's come to help with supper."

Molly turned, her smile widening as she caught sight of him. "Hello, Elijah. I was beginning to think you'd run off to join a cattle drive."

He cleared his throat, willing his voice to remain steady. "Takes more than a long day's work to keep me away from a good meal." He stepped farther into the kitchen. "Though I didn't expect such fine company."

"Oh, I'm sure you say the same to all the ladies who wander into your kitchen." Molly's eyes twinkled with mischief.

Lilian snorted, earning her a mock glare from Molly. The easy banter between them warmed Elijah's heart, even as he struggled to keep his own emotions in check.

"Only the ones who can handle a rolling pin without causing injury," he retorted, moving to wash his hands at the sink. As he passed Molly, he caught a whiff of lavender and sunshine, a scent he was beginning to associate with her.

"And how do you know I haven't?" Molly challenged, brandishing the rolling pin. "I'll have you know, I'm quite dangerous in the kitchen."

Elijah raised an eyebrow, fighting back a smile. "Is that so? Should I be worried about the safety of our supper, then?"

Molly's laughter filled the kitchen. "Your mother's been keeping a close eye on me. I think the meal will survive my presence."

As they continued their playful back-and-forth, Elijah marveled at how natural it felt to have Molly there, in his home, surrounded by his family. He found himself relaxing, the tension of the day's work melting away in the warmth of her presence.

Yet, even as he enjoyed their easy conversation, a part of him held back, ever mindful of the temporary nature of her stay. He couldn't let himself get too attached, couldn't let her see how glad he was to see her.

As Molly's eyes met his, Elijah wondered if he was fighting a losing battle against his own heart.

Chapter Seventeen

The Beckett family gathered around the weathered oak table, plates piled high with steaming stew and fresh-baked biscuits. Laughter filled the air, punctuated by the clink of silverware against ceramic. Molly sat between Elijah's sisters, her eyes glistening as she regaled them with tales of past newspaper articles.

"And then," Molly said, barely containing her mirth, "the mayor's prize pig escaped right in the middle of his speech."

The table erupted in laughter. Even Elijah joined in with a deep chuckle. He found his gaze drawn to Molly, marveling at how she fit with his family. Her presence seemed to soften the rough edges of their frontier life.

"Molly, dear," Naomi said. "You must write about this for the Mystic Gazette. I'm sure Faith would love to publish it."

Elijah nodded in agreement. "You've got a real talent for storytelling, Molly. I'm sure Faith will recognize it."

As soon as the words left his mouth, Elijah tensed, worried he'd revealed too much. Busying himself with his plate of stew, he stole glances at Molly from beneath his lashes. The candlelight caught the gold in her hair, and he found himself wanting to slide his fingers through each strand.

"Elijah Beckett," Molly teased, her eyes twinkling. "Was that almost a compliment?"

He cleared his throat, fighting the urge to reach across the table and take her hand. "Just stating facts, Miss O'Sullivan. No need to get a big head about it."

His siblings snickered, and Elijah felt a flush creeping up his neck. He'd never been one for flowery words or grand gestures, but something about Molly made him want to try.

As the meal progressed, he found himself leaning in whenever Molly spoke, hanging on her every word. He caught himself pushing the last biscuit onto her plate, earning a raised eyebrow from his observant mother.

"Molly, how long do you plan on staying in Mystic?" Grayson asked.

The question hung in the air, and Elijah felt his heart skip a beat. He held his breath, waiting for her answer, all the while scolding himself for caring so much.

Molly's eyes met Elijah's across the table, and for a moment, the rest of the world seemed to fade away. "Well, I'm finding I quite like it here. I might stick around for a while."

As the family dispersed after supper, Elijah found himself wandering out to the porch, his mind a whirlwind of conflicting thoughts. The evening air was cool against his skin, carrying the scent of grass and distant pine. He leaned against the railing, his gaze fixed on the darkening horizon.

"Penny for your thoughts?" Molly's voice startled him from his reverie.

Elijah turned, drinking in the sight of her silhouetted against the light spilling from the house. "Might not be worth much," he replied, his tone gruff.

She stepped closer, her skirts rustling softly. "Oh, I doubt that. You Becketts are full of surprises."

He chuckled, a low rumble in his chest. "That so?"

"Mmhmm," she hummed, joining him at the railing. "For instance, I never pegged you for a biscuit thief."

He felt heat creep up his neck. "I don't know what you're talking about."

"Sure you don't." She bumped her shoulder against his.

The casual touch sent a jolt through him, and he found himself wrestling with a surge of longing. He wanted to pull her close, to tell her how she'd upended his carefully ordered world. Instead, he gripped the railing tighter, his knuckles white.

"Molly," he began, his voice rough with emotion, "what you said at supper... about staying..."

She turned to face him, her expression serious. "I meant it. I know I came here just to take photographs, but..." She paused, searching his face. "There's something about this place. About the people."

His heart thundered in his chest. "The people, huh?"

Her lips curved into a soft smile. "Some more than others."

They stood there, the air between them charged with unspoken possibilities. He found himself leaning in, drawn by an irresistible force. Her eyes fluttered closed, her breath catching.

"Eli!" The screen door banged open. "Ma needs help with the—" Annalee's voice cut off abruptly. "Oh! I'm sorry. I didn't mean to interrupt."

Elijah straightened, clearing his throat. "You didn't," he answered, even as his pulse raced. He glanced at Molly, saw the flush on her cheeks, the slight tremble of her hand as she tucked a strand of hair behind her ear.

"I should go help your mother," Molly murmured.

As she brushed past him, her fingers grazed his arm, leaving a trail of fire in their wake. Elijah watched her go, a mix of frustration and hope surging through him. He turned back to the darkening land, his future suddenly seeming as vast and full of possibility as the Montana sky.

Elijah's gaze lingered on the horizon, his mind a whirlwind of conflicting emotions. The ranch stretched before him, a reminder of his responsibilities and the life he'd always known. Yet Molly's presence had awakened something in him, a yearning for more than the familiar rhythms of ranch life.

He turned back to the house, his steps carrying him inside. Laughter drifted from the kitchen, Molly's melodious voice blending with his mother's and Annalee's. The sound tugged at something deep within him.

He paused in the doorway, drinking in the scene. Molly stood at the sink, her sleeves rolled up, hands submerged in soapy water. She glanced over her shoulder, catching his eye, and a smile bloomed on her face.

"Well, don't just stand there," Naomi chided. "Come make yourself useful, Elijah."

He moved to Molly's side, reaching for a dishtowel. "Yes, ma'am."

As they worked side by side, Elijah found himself hyper-aware of Molly's every movement. The brush of her arm against his sent sparks through his body. He struggled to keep his focus on the task at hand.

"Your mother's cooking puts even the finest Chicago restaurants to shame," Molly said, putting a few inches of distance between her and Elijah.

"Ma has always had a way with a skillet. Though I reckon you've eaten at fancier establishments than our humble ranch kitchen."

She laughed. "Oh, you'd be surprised. I've eaten at all kinds of places during my life."

His lips twitched in what might have been the ghost of a smile. He found himself oddly at ease in

Molly's presence, despite his usual aversion to talkative folk. There was something refreshing about her candor, her ability to fill the silence without making it feel forced.

As he reached for another dish, he couldn't help noticing the way Molly's hands moved with practiced efficiency. For all her big city upbringing, she wasn't afraid of a little hard work. It was admirable.

"You handle those dishes like a pro," he observed.

"I'll have you know, even Chicago debutantes can roll up their sleeves when the occasion calls for it."

Before he could respond, the kitchen door swung open, and Naomi Beckett strode in. "Elijah." Her voice carried the no-nonsense tone that had kept the Beckett clan in line for decades. "I've made up the guest room. Molly will be staying the night."

His eyebrows rose a fraction, but he kept his surprise in check. "That so?" he asked, glancing at Molly.

She nodded, a hint of color rising to her cheeks. "If it's not too much trouble, Mrs. Beckett. I'd hate to impose."

"Nonsense," Naomi replied, waving away the concern. "It's too late for a lady to be riding back to town alone."

Elijah dried his hands on a nearby towel, his mind working through this unexpected development. Something in his chest tightened at the thought.

"Well then, how about we take a walk before turning in, Molly? If you're amenable."

"Sounds lovely."

Elijah caught his mother's knowing look as they

left the kitchen. He straightened his shoulders, determined not to let her see how Molly's presence affected him. As they stepped outside, Elijah couldn't shake the feeling something significant was going on between them.

They made their way toward the new corral. Elijah's boots crunched on the packed earth, while beside him, Molly's shorter steps matched his pace, her presence a warm counterpoint to the cool night air.

Clearing his throat, he broke the comfortable silence. "What was it like, growing up in Chicago?"

"It was certainly different from Montana. The city is always alive, always moving. Nothing like the peace out here."

Elijah nodded, trying to picture the bustling city. He'd grown up on the ranch, never traveling more than a few hundred miles away to drive their cattle to market.

Approaching the corral, he found himself wanting to know more. It was an unfamiliar feeling for the taciturn rancher.

"Tell me more about Chicago," he said.

Molly's eyes lit up with enthusiasm as she began to describe her beloved hometown. "The energy there is unlike anything you've ever experienced. You should see the lumberyards along the river. Stacks of timber as far as the eye can see."

"Sounds like quite a sight."

"The Union Stockyard is enormous," Molly said, her voice filled with a mix of awe and nostalgia.

"Father told me the stockyard was over four hundred acres, and covered with pens, railroad chutes, and office buildings. It's impressive."

Watching the horses inside the corral, he found himself captivated by her descriptions. He'd never given much thought to city life, knowing he'd never want to live in one. Her words did paint a vivid picture. "What about the wheat farming around Chicago? I heard it's big business back there."

"The grain elevators are enormous, Elijah. Father said Chicago's become the wheat capital of the world. It's incredible to see the ships and trains coming and going, all laden with golden grain."

He nodded, impressed by the scale of it all. He was about to ask another question when her excitement seemed to surge anew.

"Oh! And have you ever heard of Montgomery Ward?"

"Can't say that I have," he admitted.

"It's this amazing mail-order catalog," she explained, her words tumbling out faster now. "You can order almost anything you can imagine. Clothes, tools, kitchen tables. Even ranch equipment!"

Elijah tilted his head, skeptical. "Ranch equipment? Through the mail?"

"Yes. They come in pieces, and you assemble them yourself. But that's not all..."

As she launched into a detailed list of the catalog's offerings, he found himself torn between amusement at her excitement and a growing sense of interest in the world beyond his ranch.

"They even offer some new-fangled bicycles." Her cheeks were flushed with enthusiasm. "Can you imagine riding one of those out here on the prairie?"

"I think I'll stick to my horse."

He leaned against the fence, his mind whirling with all the information Molly had shared. His hard disposition began to crack at her genuine pleasure in sharing information about her hometown. Her enthusiasm was infectious, and he found himself smiling despite his usual reserved nature. The way her eyes lit up as she spoke stirred something within him, a curiosity about the world beyond Wild Spirit Ranch he'd rarely allowed himself to indulge.

"Chicago also has some truly magnificent museums and art galleries."

He raised an eyebrow, intrigued. "Art galleries? I can't say I've ever been to one of those."

Her face brightened. "They're wonderful. There's so much to see, it can take a full day."

Elijah marveled at how easy their conversation had become. He'd never been one for idle chatter, but with Molly, the words seemed to flow naturally. It was a strange feeling.

She nudged his arm. "You know, Elijah Beckett, you simply must visit Chicago someday. It would be quite the adventure."

"And what would a rancher do in a big city like Chicago?"

"There's so much. The architecture alone would leave you breathless. And the restaurants. You wouldn't be bored."

As they turned from the corral, he found himself considering the possibility. He'd never been one for travel, content with the vast expanse of his ranch. Something about the way she described it made him curious.

"Sounds like you miss it."

Her steps slowed. "I suppose. In some ways. The energy of the city, the constant bustle and excitement. It's quite different from Mystic."

He nodded, waiting for her to continue, sensing there was more she wanted to say.

"But there are things I don't miss. The expectations, the endless social engagements, the..." She trailed off, hesitating.

"The what?"

Molly sighed, a rueful smile crossing her face. "The suitors my father encourages. Due to my father's efforts, I had no shortage of men vying for my attention. None of them interested me."

Elijah felt a strange tightness in his chest at her words. "Were the suitors the reason you came out here?"

She shook her head. "Not to escape, exactly. More to find something real. Something genuine. What about you, Elijah? Have there been any women in your past?"

His jaw tightened. He hadn't expected the conversation to turn in this direction, and he found himself caught off guard. "There was one."

Chapter Eighteen

"Oh?" Molly prompted.

Elijah took a deep breath. "Her name was Laura." The words felt strange on his tongue. It had been years since he'd spoken her name. "I thought we'd marry someday."

Molly's expression softened, encouraging him to continue. His gaze drifted to the distant mountains, silhouetted against the night sky. "We met when we were thirteen. Grew up together, and fell in love over the years. At least, I thought we did."

Continuing their walk, Elijah found himself opening up more than he had in years. He told Molly about stolen moments with Laura behind the schoolhouse, about their shared dreams of building a life together on Wild Spirit Ranch. With each word, he felt a weight lifting from his shoulders, even as the old pain resurfaced.

"What happened?"

Elijah's eyes clouded over, his jaw clenching. "She left." The words hung heavy in the air between them.

"Why did she leave, Elijah?"

His steps slowed as they continued around the barn. "It's not something I talk about," he muttered, more to himself than to Molly.

Her shoulder brushed against his arm. "Mother told me talking about the past can help us understand the present."

His gaze remained fixed on the distant mountains. Steeling himself, he released a deep breath.

"Laura wanted more than Mystic could offer. Said she felt suffocated here. She needed to see the world beyond these mountains."

She nodded, encouraging him to go on.

"I offered to take her traveling, show her other places," he continued, a hint of bitterness creeping into his voice. "But it wasn't just about seeing new sights. She wanted a different life altogether. One without me in it."

The pain in his voice was palpable. Molly placed her hand on his arm, feeling Elijah tense for a moment before relaxing.

"I can't even imagine how much her plans hurt you."

His jaw clenched, unable to meet her gaze. "It made me realize how opening yourself up to someone leaves you vulnerable."

As he spoke, a coyote's mournful howl echoed across the valley, sending a shiver down Molly's spine. The sound seemed to underscore the loneliness in Elijah's words, and she found herself wondering what it would take to break through the walls he'd built around his heart.

Her hand remained on Elijah's arm. She looked up at him.

"Don't you think closing yourself off might mean missing out on something wonderful?"

His gaze met hers, his expression unreadable. "Maybe," he conceded after a moment. "But the risk isn't something I want to repeat."

"Life's full of risks, Elijah. Back in Chicago, I took a risk leaving everything I knew behind. And look where it's led me."

A hint of a smile tugged at the corner of Elijah's mouth. "To a dusty ranch in the middle of nowhere?"

Molly laughed, the sound bright in the stillness of the night. "To adventure. To new experiences. To meeting people I never would have otherwise."

Something stirred within him, a warmth he hadn't experienced in years. He cleared his throat, aware of how close they were standing.

"You've got a way of putting things."

She grinned. "It's a gift."

Their gazes met, though neither spoke.

As they stood there, the distant sound of a horse neighing broke the silence. Elijah's posture straightened, his rancher's instincts kicking in.

"We should head back," he said, but there was a reluctance in his tone that hadn't been there before.

As they took the steps to the front door, Elijah paused, turning to face Molly. "Thank you," he said simply, but his eyes conveyed more than his words.

"For what?"

"For listening," he replied.

As they stood there, the sound of rapid hoofbeats filled the air. Elijah's head snapped up, his body tensing. A rider was approaching, and even in the dim light, Elijah could see the urgency in the man's posture.

"Something's wrong." His hand moved to Molly's arm as if to protect her from whatever news was galloping toward them.

The rider came into view, his hat pulled low, shielding his face. As he pulled up in front of the porch, he lifted his face to stare into his younger brother's shocked gaze. Elijah took a step forward.

"Cody?"

"Hello, Eli." He swung to the ground, tossing the reins over the post.

Bounding down the steps, Elijah tugged him into a hug, slapping his back. Pulling back, he looked over the brother who'd left years earlier.

"It's darn good to see you."

Before Cody could respond, the front door slammed open. Grayson walked outside, followed by Joshua. The two came to an abrupt stop, their gazes locked on the brother who'd been gone much too long.

Joshua reacted first, flying down the steps to hug his older brother. Behind him, Grayson stood on the edge of the porch. When Joshua pulled away, Cody looked up at his older brother. His gaze didn't waver as he took the steps up to the porch.

"Grayson."

"Cody. Been a while."

"Can't argue that."

"You visiting or planning to stay?"

"I'm staying."

Grayson reached out, settling a broad hand on his brother's shoulder. "Welcome home."

Cody and his family sat around the dining room table, drinking coffee while they peppered him with questions. Beside him, his mother, Naomi, sat rigid in her chair, dabbing at her eyes.

"Did you find the men?" Joshua asked. No one asked which men. It was understood Cody left the ranch to locate those who'd murdered his wife and daughter.

"Yes."

"Did a jury convict them?" Annalee asked.

Cody stared into his cup, giving a slight nod. "Justice was done."

As the questions continued, Grayson leaned back in his chair and listened. He already knew what happened to the killers. Had known for a long time. It was something he hadn't shared with anyone, not even Jolene.

Beside him, Elijah listened, contributing little. Unlike Grayson, he only had suspicions of what happened to the three men who'd taken so much from the Becketts. Over the years, Elijah had come to rely on his instincts.

An hour passed before Cody stood to stretch, followed by a wide yawn. "I'm exhausted." He set a hand on his mother's shoulder. "Do I still have the same bedroom?"

"Nothing has changed."

"All right. See you all in the morning." He walked to the stairs, taking them at a slow pace while the others shot glances at each other.

Grayson stood next. "I'm going to bed, too."

"You just want to see that cute baby of yours," Annalee teased.

"And your beautiful wife," Parker added.

A smile curved Grayson's mouth. "Yes to both."

The others filed upstairs within minutes, leaving Molly and Elijah at the table. "Do you want more coffee?" she asked.

"Nah. I've had enough."

When she stood, he reached out to grab her hand. "Stay for a bit."

"All right." She sat back down, shifting to face him. He continued to hold her hand as the silence stretched for several minutes, him staring at their joined hands.

"Cody left while Grayson was gone. Their being gone made me the oldest. Ma looked at me to help keep everyone going. We got into a routine. All went well until Grayson returned with Jolene. The others didn't know who to listen to regarding chores. It took a while before everything smoothed out. Grayson became the big boss while I made sure every day work was getting done. Now..."

"You're wondering what will happen now with Cody's return."

He gave a slow nod. "I don't know how I'll fit in. This ranch has been my life." Elijah looked at her. "It's in my blood. Grayson returned in order to be close to family. He never had the pull to ranch. He's gotten more into it over the last two years, and we've found a good way to work together. Cody's different. He loves ranching as much as me. At least, he used to."

She waited, sensing there was more Elijah wanted to say. After a bit, he continued.

"Maybe it's time for me to carve out my place."

"Your own place?"

"Before he died, Pa made it clear each of his children would be given their own acreage for a house. Ma reminded me of it after Grayson returned. She believed he'd want to build his own place. He surprised all of us by staying here. We all love Jolene, and now with the baby, Ma would have a hard time if they left. Maybe I'm the one who should build a house."

Molly didn't know how much to say. It was his life, after all. She was here as a guest.

"What do you think?" He squeezed her hand.

"Maybe you should give it some time. Right now, you don't know what Cody wants."

"Might be best."

Several minutes passed before Molly slipped her hand from his and stood. "I'm going to head upstairs to bed. Are you going to be all right?"

A wry grin formed. "Me? Yes, I'll be fine." Rising, he began picking up the dirty cups.

She helped, offering to wash them. When finished, she dried her hands. "Well, have a good night, Elijah."

He reached out, slinking an arm around her waist to draw her close. Before he could think about it too much, he lowered his head, brushing a kiss across her lips. When she didn't back away, he pressed his mouth to hers.

Lifting his head, he took a step away. "Goodnight, Molly. Sleep well."

Chapter Nineteen

The leaves of the cottonwoods rustled in the gentle Montana breeze as Molly hefted her bulky equipment box onto the back of the buggy. She secured it with practiced efficiency, her nimble fingers working the straps and buckles with ease.

"I can't thank you enough for your hospitality," she said, turning to face Naomi and Elijah, who stood a few feet away. Her eyes glistened with genuine warmth as she met each of their gazes.

Elijah stepped forward, his rugged features softening into a smile. "You're welcome to stay longer." He reached around her to check the straps on her equipment, his fingers brushing against her arm.

She felt a flutter in her chest at the slight touch but tamped it down. Molly hadn't meant to fall for the handsome cowboy, yet she had.

"I want to develop the plates and see if my order for additional plates arrived at the mercantile." She tossed her braid over her shoulder.

"Perhaps you'll return. For more photographs, I

mean," he said as he helped her into the buggy. "Be careful, Molly. Danger can come at any time, from any direction." Elijah squeezed her hand before stepping away.

With a final wave, Molly flicked the reins and set off down the trail toward Mystic. As the ranch faded into the distance behind her, the vast Montana landscape unfurled before her eyes like a living painting.

Rolling hills of golden grass stretched as far as the eye could see, punctuated by stands of evergreens and jagged, snowcapped peaks on the horizon. Molly's breath caught in her throat at the sheer majesty of it all.

She shot another look over her shoulder, realizing she already missed Elijah. Minutes after leaving, she wanted to turn the buggy around.

Molly refocused on the beauty around her in an effort to shove away thoughts of Elijah. She noticed how the sunlight danced across the waving grass, creating a glistening sea of gold.

As she guided the buggy along the winding trail, she thought of all her plans. Her fingers itched to capture the raw beauty of this land with her camera.

A sudden gust of wind whipped strands of hair around her face, and she laughed out loud, relishing the feeling of freedom coursing through her veins. This was why she'd left her family and Chicago behind. She'd ached to experience life in all its wild, unrestrained glory.

As the buggy crested a hill, she caught sight of a

fork in the trail. Certain Mystic was to her right, she followed her instincts. Within minutes, she realized nothing looked familiar.

Looking for a place to turn the buggy around, the landscape opened up into a breathtaking vista she hadn't seen before. A hidden gem tucked away in the vastness of Mystic Valley. Rolling hills cascaded down to a winding river framed by vast grasslands and jagged mountains.

Molly stared in wonder, pulling the buggy to a stop. With practiced efficiency, she hopped down and retrieved her camera equipment. Her fingers trembled with excitement as she set everything up, her mind already composing the perfect shot.

"Just imagine what Papa would say if he could see me now." She chuckled. "His obstinate little Molly, out here in the wild, capturing the untamed beauty of—"

A twig snapped behind her, and she froze. The hairs on the back of her neck stood up as she slowly turned around, her heart pounding. She found herself face-to-face with a group of Indians on horseback, their expressions unreadable as they regarded her with curiosity and wariness.

Molly swallowed hard, considering her situation. She straightened her spine, channeling every ounce of her outgoing nature and Chicago upbringing.

"Good day, gentlemen," she said, her voice steadier than she felt. "I'm Molly O'Sullivan. I hope I'm not trespassing on your land. I'm a photographer, you see, and I couldn't resist capturing this stunning view."

She gestured to her camera, maintaining eye contact with who she assumed was the leader. The silence stretched between them, taut as a bowstring.

"Do you speak English?" Molly asked. "Parlez-vous français, perhaps?" She wracked her brain for the few words of Lakota she'd picked up from a book, hoping it might be close enough to their language.

As the Indians continued to stare at her, she struggled with possible outcomes. Would they view her as a threat? As she opened her mouth to try again, the leader urged his mount forward, his gaze fixed on her camera.

The leader's attention shifted from the camera to Molly's face, his expression softening slightly. "We are Crow," he said in English.

Molly's shoulders relaxed, relief washing over her. "Crow," she repeated, a smile spreading across her face. "I've read about your people. Your horsemanship is legendary."

The man's eyebrows raised, surprise flickering in his dark eyes. "You know of us?"

"Only what I've read," she admitted. "I'd love to learn more, if you're willing to share."

The leader conferred briefly with his companions in their native tongue before turning back to her. "I am Plenty Bear. What brings you to the land of Becketts, Molly O'Sullivan?"

She gestured to her camera, stifling her surprise at hearing the Beckett name. "I'm a photographer. I preserve places and people for history." She paused, an idea forming. "Would you allow me to take your photograph? To show the world the proud spirit of the Crow?"

Plenty Bear's eyes narrowed, considering. "What would you do with this photograph?"

"I'd use it to educate others about your people," she explained, her voice filled with passion. "To show your strength, your dignity. Too many have false ideas about Indians."

The group murmured among themselves, and Molly held her breath. Finally, Plenty Bear nodded. "We will allow this. First, you will tell us of your world, a woman who travels alone."

She began to speak of Chicago, of her journey west, watching as the Crow warriors listened with rapt attention. Plenty Bear asked a few questions, then nodded when satisfied. Molly began positioning them for the photograph.

"Stand there, please," she directed, pointing to a spot where the light caught Plenty Bear's proud profile.

As she worked, Molly felt a growing connection with these people. Their faces, once wary, now showed curiosity, and even amusement at her enthusiastic directions.

She hummed with excitement as she adjusted the focus on her camera. The Crow Indians stood before her, their faces a mixture of curiosity and pride. Plenty Bear, their leader, stood tall in the center, his eagle feather headdress catching the sunlight.

"Hold still, please," she called out, her voice

steady despite her nerves.

With practiced precision, Molly exposed the first plate. The camera's shutter clicked, capturing the essence of the Crow men in a single instant. Without missing a beat, she swiftly changed the plate and repositioned herself slightly.

"One more," she announced.

As she prepared to take the second photograph, Molly noticed a shift in the group's behavior. Their poses became more relaxed, yet somehow more powerful. Plenty Bear's eyes seemed to look beyond the camera.

Click. The second exposure was complete.

She emerged from behind her camera, a triumphant smile on her face. "Thank you," she said, her voice filled with genuine gratitude. "These images will tell your story for generations to come."

As she turned to pack up her equipment, a movement in her peripheral vision caught her attention. She whirled around, her eyes widening in surprise. There, not fifty yards away, stood Grayson, Cody, and Elijah. They were watching her, amused smiles playing on their lips.

Her cheeks flushed with a mix of embarrassment and indignation. How long had they been there? She straightened her back, determined not to show her discomfort.

"Hello, gentlemen. Enjoying the show?"

The Becketts exchanged glances before dismounting their horses. Grayson, the eldest, took the lead as they approached the gathering. His imposing presence softened as he greeted the Crow men with a respectful nod.

"Plenty Bear," Grayson said, his voice carrying a mix of familiarity and deference. "It's good to see you and your people. I hope the grazing has been plentiful this season."

Cody, hard-bitten and taciturn, surprised her by engaging in conversation with some of the Crow men. His blue eyes, often clouded, seemed to lighten as he gestured, discussing what appeared to be hunting techniques.

Elijah, however, headed straight to Molly. As he approached, she felt her heart quicken, remembering the way he'd held her in his arms and kissed her before heading to bed last night.

"Molly. Are you lost?"

She raised an eyebrow. "Not at all. I'm quite capable of handling myself. Though I admit, I didn't expect to stumble upon such gracious subjects for my photography."

His lips twitched. "We were riding to town when Cody spotted wagon tracks veering off on this trail. Curious, we took it. Then we spotted you. Thought we'd make sure you were safe, given the unexpected company."

"The Crow men have been nothing but welcoming. I've learned more about their culture in this brief encounter than I could have from any book."

He nodded, his expression unreadable. "That may be so, but these hills can be treacherous for those unfamiliar with them. It's easy to lose your way."

When she opened her mouth to retort, Molly realized with a start she wasn't sure which trail would lead her back to Mystic.

"We can escort you to town if you'd like," he offered.

"Thank you, Elijah."

As they bid farewell to the Crow, the group set off, with Elijah riding alongside Molly's buggy while Cody and Grayson took up positions ahead of them.

"Your family seems to have quite the rapport with the local Crow tribe."

Elijah's gaze remained fixed on the trail ahead. "We've shared these lands for generations."

"In Chicago, such relationships seem to be more contentious."

"This isn't Chicago, Molly. Out here, you learn to judge folk by their actions, not their origins."

As they approached Mystic, the conversation lulled, allowing her to reflect on the day's events. The Becketts' protective nature, while sometimes grating, now struck her as comforting.

Upon reaching town, Elijah dismounted, moving to help Molly down from the buggy. His strong hands encircled her waist, and for a brief moment, their eyes met. Molly felt a flutter in her chest and her face heat, again recalling their kiss.

"I'll help you unload." Elijah reached for her equipment box.

"That's really not necessary—" she began, but he'd already lifted the heavy case with ease. "I want to see if my order is waiting for me at the mercantile."

As they walked, Molly found herself studying Elijah's profile. His jaw was set in its usual stern line, but there was something in his eyes—a warmth she'd come to expect when they were together.

The bell above the mercantile door jingled as they entered. Casper Jennings looked up from his ledger, a smile breaking across his weathered face.

"Miss O'Sullivan. Afternoon, Elijah. What perfect timing. Your dry plates just arrived on today's stage."

"Oh, that's wonderful news!"

As Casper retrieved her order, Molly turned to Elijah. "This is splendid. The additional plates will allow me to capture even more of this magnificent land."

For a moment, his indifferent facade cracked, revealing a hint of a smile. "Reckon there's plenty out there worth capturing."

"Here you are." Casper set the crate of dry plates on the counter.

"Thank you, Mr. Jennings. May I use the room you set up for me later today?"

"Anytime you need to."

After paying, Elijah hefted the crate of dry plates with ease, settling it on his shoulder before picking up the camera equipment, his muscled arms barely straining under the weight.

"Where to?"

"The Mystic Hotel."

"What did Casper mean about the room?"

She smiled. "He set up a room in the back for me to develop my plates. Mr. Jennings is fascinated by photography. He doesn't even charge me for the room's use."

As they walked along the boardwalk to the hotel, Molly found herself unduly aware of his presence beside her. The silence between them charged with a feeling she couldn't define.

"I appreciate your help," she ventured, glancing sideways at him.

"It's nothing."

When they reached the hotel, he followed her up the narrow staircase to her room. As she fumbled with the key, she could feel the warmth radiating from his body so close behind her.

Inside the room, Elijah set the equipment box and crate down carefully on the floor.

As he moved them out of the way, she found herself studying the lines of his back, the way his shirt stretched across his broad shoulders.

Elijah straightened, catching her gaze. For a moment, something intense flickered in his eyes, making Molly's breath catch in her throat.

"I have errands to complete. Afterward, do you have time to join me for lunch?" he asked, his voice low and husky.

Molly swallowed hard, her heart pounding. "Yes, I do."

He nodded once, then strode to the door. As he reached for the handle, he paused, looking back at her. "I won't be gone long."

And then he was out the door, leaving Molly alone with her racing thoughts and the sudden, overwhelming realization she was falling in love with Elijah Beckett.

Chapter Twenty

Molly sank onto the edge of her bed, her mind whirling with conflicting emotions. The room felt suddenly empty without Elijah's presence, yet his lingering scent, a mix of leather, pine, and something uniquely him, filled her senses.

"What am I doing?" she whispered to herself. The happiness of realizing her feelings for Elijah warred with the pragmatism she'd depended on to guide her life.

She stood, pacing the small confines of her room. "I came here to build my career, not to fall for a rancher," she muttered.

A knock at the door startled her from her reverie. "Miss O'Sullivan?" It was Faith Goodell, the owner of the Mystic Gazette. "May I have a word?"

Molly composed herself before opening the door. "Of course, Faith. Please, come in."

As Faith entered, Molly noticed the woman's eyes dart to the crate of dry plates, then back to her. "I hope I'm not intruding."

"Not at all. Why don't we go downstairs to talk? I believe there is coffee in the parlor."

"Of course." Faith headed into the hall, with Molly a few steps behind.

Once the two had poured coffee and found seats, Molly leaned forward. "What can I do for you?"

"Well, this may sound presumptuous, but I wanted to ask if you might work for the Mystic Gazette as a reporter. The town is growing, and I'm finding it hard to keep up."

Molly pushed aside her personal turmoil as she considered the surprise offer. "I must say, you've caught me by surprise. It's a fascinating offer. You do know I plan to travel to Yellowstone, then continue west to the Pacific Ocean?"

"Yes, I know." Faith leaned forward. "I understand you have a relationship with a newspaper in Chicago. If you aren't tied to them on an exclusive contract, I'd hoped you might consider traveling as a reporter for my paper."

Molly's heart rate quickened. Here was an opportunity to further her career in an unexpected way. "Your offer is quite intriguing. To clarify, I send my contact at the paper my article and photographs through the mail. They've been very good about including them when space permits. However, there is nothing exclusive." She thought for a moment, taking a sip of coffee before setting the cup down. "I don't see a reason not to be associated with your newspaper."

"Wonderful. When you have time, please come by

the office, and we'll write out the details."

"I'll stop by this afternoon." Molly's lips tilted up at the corners. "And thank you for the opportunity."

As Faith stood to leave, Molly felt a tremor of excitement roll through her. Wasn't this exactly why she'd come to Montana? To prove herself as a serious photographer and journalist?

Taking the stairs to her room, Molly's gaze landed on the crate Elijah had so carefully carried for her. She couldn't wait to tell him about Faith's offer.

Elijah and Molly strolled down Mystic's boardwalk toward the Golden Griddle, her steps were a lively bounce with barely contained excitement. She cast frequent glances at Elijah, as if bursting to share a secret.

Ever observant, he noticed the spring in Molly's step and the way she kept looking at him. His brows furrowed as he tried to decipher her mood.

"You're in good spirits," he remarked. "Something you want to tell me?"

Her cheeks flushed. "It's nothing. Just enjoying this beautiful day." She gestured at the clear Montana sky.

His eyes narrowed skeptically. Elijah had grown up reading cattle and horses. Reading people wasn't much different. "Uh-huh," he grunted, unconvinced.

As they approached the restaurant, Molly's stomach growled, and she laughed, patting it. "I guess I'm hungrier than I realized."

Elijah held the door for her, a ghost of a smile tugging at his lips. "After you."

She swept past him, her skirt swishing. She paused inside, drinking in the warm, inviting atmosphere of the Golden Griddle. "Smells wonderful," she breathed.

He shrugged, uncomfortable with her enthusiasm. "Always does."

She shot him a glance. "You're impossible sometimes."

As they settled onto chairs at a table in the middle of the room, Elijah found himself studying Molly. There was something different about her. Her eyes danced with suppressed joy, and she couldn't seem to sit still.

"All right. What's got you so stirred up?"

Molly fidgeted with her napkin. "Is it that obvious?"

Elijah's lips quirked into a half-smile. "About as subtle as a stampede."

She bit her lip, debating whether to spill her news. "It's silly, really. You probably won't even care."

Elijah leaned back, crossing his arms. "Tell me."

She laughed, the sound bright and clear in the bustling restaurant. "Oh, very well. If you must know, Faith Goodell made me an offer today. She wants me to contribute articles and photographs to the Mystic Gazette." Her eyes shone with enthusiasm.

His gaze narrowed, but before Elijah could respond, a waitress bustled up to their table. "What'll it be, dears?"

Molly glanced at the chalkboard menu. "The elk stew sounds wonderful. And some fresh bread, please."

"Make that two," Elijah added.

Moments later, two steaming bowls arrived, accompanied by thick slices of crusty bread still warm from the oven. Molly dipped her spoon into the hearty stew, watching the steam rise. She took a bite and closed her eyes in bliss.

"It's perfect," she murmured. "The meat melts in your mouth."

Elijah raised an eyebrow at her poetic description but said nothing as he tucked into his own meal. As they ate, Molly couldn't contain her excitement any longer.

"During my travels, I'll be mailing articles and photographs to Faith for the Mystic Gazette, and to my contact at the Chicago paper." She paused, her spoon hovering midair. "What do you think, Elijah? Isn't it a wonderful opportunity?"

His stony eyes fixed on Molly with such intensity she shifted uncomfortably in her seat. The enthusiasm bubbling within her began to waver under his serious gaze.

"It's certainly an opportunity," he said finally, his voice measured and devoid of the excitement Molly had hoped to hear. He set down his spoon. "How often would you be sending these articles?"

She searched his features, trying to read the emotions behind his impassive features. "Well, I was thinking maybe once or twice a month to start. It all depends on what I find fascinating enough to write about, with photographs, so people can visualize the story as they read."

He nodded, his jaw tightening. "And these photographs you mentioned. What sort of things would you be capturing?"

"Oh, all sorts." Her voice rose with renewed enthusiasm despite Elijah's lack of it. "The beautiful landscapes, the daily life of the townsfolk, maybe even the troubles faced with ranching work."

"I see," he said, his tone flat. "And you'd be sending these pictures back east as well?"

Molly's heart sank at his continued lack of excitement. She found herself desperately wishing she could peer into his thoughts to understand what was going on behind those inscrutable eyes.

"Yes, that's the idea. Elijah, what do you really think about all this? I can't quite tell how you feel about it."

The waitress approached their table, her arrival a welcome interruption to the growing tension. "Can I interest you folks in some dessert? There are peach pies cooling on the rack." Her cheerful voice was a stark contrast to the atmosphere between them.

Molly seized the opportunity, forcing a smile. "Yes, please. I'll have a slice of peach pie and coffee."

He didn't shift his gaze from Molly's when he spoke. "I'll have the same."

As the waitress bustled away, he leaned back in

his chair, his posture rigid.

Molly clasped her hands in her lap, fighting to retain her enthusiasm. "Peach is my favorite."

Silence descended upon them once more, broken only by the clinking of cutlery from nearby tables. She cleared her throat, desperate to break the unease.

"You didn't answer my question, Elijah. What do you think about Faith's offer?"

"It's an interesting opportunity." His voice remained flat.

The waitress returned with their dessert and cups of coffee. The aroma of peach pie wafted between them. Neither made a move to pick up their forks.

Molly felt a knot forming in her stomach. She'd been so excited about the prospect of sharing her experiences. "Showing the beauty and reality of life out here would be a good thing. Wouldn't it?"

Elijah's jaw tightened. "I suppose so."

The tension between them was palpable now, hanging in the air like a thundercloud ready to burst. She found herself gripping the coffee cup so tight her knuckles turned white. She wanted to make him understand, but something held her back.

As they sat there, peach pie untouched and coffee growing cold, Molly couldn't shake the feeling this conversation was about more than Faith's offer. Something deeper was brewing beneath the surface, threatening to change everything between them.

He cleared his throat, his eyes flickering to the window before settling back on Molly. "I've got a heap of work to do at the ranch. This is the busiest time of year. Not much time for anything else."

She blinked, thrown by the abrupt change of subject. "Elijah, what do you really think about—"

"I should head back," he interrupted, pushing his untouched pie aside. Paying for their meals, he stood and pulled out Molly's chair.

Stepping out onto the boardwalk, he walked beside her on the way to the hotel. The usual banter between them was notably absent, replaced by a heavy silence.

They passed the mercantile, its windows displaying supplies for the coming winter. It was a stark reminder of the changing seasons. Molly couldn't help wondering if the chill she felt was from the approaching winter or the growing distance between her and Elijah.

As they neared the hotel, her thoughts drifted to her camera, safely tucked away in her room. She imagined capturing this moment. The quiet streets of Mystic, the determined set of Elijah's shoulders, the unspoken tension hanging between them. But some moments, she realized, were too complex, too raw to be contained in a single image.

Elijah came to an abrupt halt in front of the Mystic Hotel, his gaze fixed on the livery stable across the way. "It's time I rode back to the ranch."

Her heart sank. She searched his face, hoping for some hint of regret or a suggestion of when they might meet again, but found only quiet resolve. "Will you be returning to town again soon?"

He shrugged, his gaze still avoiding hers. "Can't

say."

A knot formed in her stomach, a physical manifestation of the loss she felt. She wanted to reach out, to make him understand the opportunity before her. The words stuck in her throat.

"Safe travels, Elijah," she said finally, forcing a smile.

He tipped his hat, a ghost of a smile on his lips. "Take care, Molly."

She stood rooted to the spot as he strode across the street toward his horse. She watched him untie the reins, his movements efficient and purposeful. As he swung into the saddle, she felt a surge of emotions. Frustration, longing, and a creeping fear she might be losing something precious before it had even begun.

Elijah turned his horse, casting one last glance in her direction. For a moment, Molly thought she saw a flicker of something in his eyes. Then he spurred his mount, and was gone, leaving Molly alone with her thoughts and the growing realization her choices might lead her down a path Elijah couldn't, or wouldn't, understand.

Chapter Twenty-One

Molly took a deep breath, steadying herself against the wave of emotions threatening to overwhelm her. With determination, she turned and entered the Mystic Hotel, her mind whirling with doubt.

As she walked toward the stairs, Faith Goodell's vibrant voice caught her attention. "Molly! I've been looking all over for you."

She plastered on a smile, pushing thoughts of Elijah to the back of her mind. "Faith, what a pleasant surprise. Is everything all right?"

Faith's eyes sparkled with excitement. "More than all right. I've received a telegram from the editor of the Helena Independent. They're interested in your photographs and stories."

"How did they know about my work?" Molly's earlier disappointment was forgotten.

"I'm friends with the owner, Don Field. I hope you don't mind, but I sent him one of your photographs and the titles of the articles you mentioned to me. He's always interested in good work from new people. Don wants to feature your work in a special edition about life in the Montana Territory." Faith's words tumbled out in a rush. "This could be a wonderful opportunity for you. Don has contacts in Seattle and along the Pacific coast."

Molly thought of the possibilities unfurling before her. "I don't know what to say. You're right. This could be an excellent opportunity."

Faith grabbed Molly's hands, squeezing them. "Say yes! Pack your bags and take the train out of Bozeman to Helena next week. You can meet with the editor and decide if this is a good fit for you."

As excitement washed over her, Molly couldn't help picturing Elijah's lukewarm enthusiasm about her ambitions. She hesitated, torn between her dreams and the pull of her heart.

"I need to think about it," Molly said, her voice barely above a whisper.

Faith's eyes showed her confusion. "Think about it? Molly, opportunities like this don't come along every day. What's holding you back?"

"I'm not sure I'm ready to go just yet," she answered.

Faith leaned forward, her gaze searching Molly's face. "Is everything all right? I thought you'd be excited about the opportunity with the Helena Independent."

She released a slow breath. "I am. There's something keeping me here in Mystic."

"Or someone?" A knowing smile tugged at Faith's lips.

"Is it that obvious?"

"Only to someone who's experienced what you have. It's Elijah Beckett, isn't it?"

Molly nodded. "I think I'm in love with him, Faith. But I don't know if he feels the same way."

"Have you talked to him about it?"

Molly shook her head. "How can I? He's so closed up and hard to read. What if I'm misreading everything?"

Faith reached out, squeezing her hand. "Elijah's not one for grand gestures. But I've seen the way he looks at you."

Hope bloomed in Molly's chest, but her doubt overshadowed it. "Even if he does feel something, would he ever act on it? He's so focused on the ranch, on his family."

"You're not exactly the type to sit around waiting for a man to make a move," Faith pointed out with a wry smile.

She laughed, some of the tension easing from her shoulders. "You're right." She glanced outside before looking back at Faith. "This is different. I don't want to push him if he's not ready."

"So, what are you going to do about Helena?"

Molly straightened in her chair, her resolve strengthening. "I think I'll send a telegram to Don Field at the Helena Independent. I can make arrangements for a visit without committing to anything long-term."

"A sound plan," Faith agreed. "It'll give you more time to figure things out with Elijah, too."

Molly stood. "I'll head over to the telegraph office.

Thank you, Faith. For listening, and for understanding."

As she reached for the door, Faith's voice stopped her. "Molly? Whatever happens, don't let fear hold you back. You're too talented, too full of life to let uncertainty keep you from pursuing your dreams."

She paused with her hand on the doorknob. Turning back to Faith, a mixture of gratitude and determination shone in her eyes. "You're right. I won't let it. For now, I'll take it one step at a time."

Molly knew her future hung in the balance. Between her growing feelings for Elijah and the promise of continuing her adventure, she struggled with what to do next.

"Molly?"

She turned back with a look of concern. "Yes?"

Faith released a deep breath, her eyes glistening with unshed tears. "I understand more than you know about your situation."

Molly's eyebrows rose in surprise. She returned to her seat, reaching out to clasp Faith's hand. "What do you mean?"

"It's Joshua," Faith whispered. "I've loved him for a long time." She shook her head. "He's never seen me as anything more than a friend."

"Oh, Faith. I had no idea. How long have you felt this way?"

Faith's gaze drifted to the window, lost in memories. "Since we were children, really. It wasn't until we grew older that I realized what those feelings meant. And now it feels like it's too late."

"It's never too late." Molly's heart ached for her

friend. "Have you ever told him how you feel?"

Faith shook her head, a rueful smile playing on her lips. "I've never had the courage. And now, after such a long time, I don't know if I ever will."

She leaned back, considering her friend's words. "You know, we're not so different, you and I. Both of us pining for men who might never return our feelings. At least we have each other to confide in."

"You're right. It helps knowing I'm not alone in this. Thank you for listening, Molly."

"What else are friends for?" Molly's eyes lit up with sudden enthusiasm. "Before I leave for Helena, I want to capture one last photograph of the mountains. Would you like to come with me?"

Faith's eyebrows lifted in surprise. "I'd love to. Unfortunately, I have too much to finish before the next edition of the Mystic Gazette."

Molly's face glowed with passion. "Someday, I want you to see them through a camera lens. The way the light plays on the peaks, the shadows in the valleys. It's like capturing a piece of heaven on earth. And who knows when I'll have another chance to photograph them."

The first rays of dawn peaked over the eastern mountains when Molly stepped out of the Mystic Hotel, her arms laden with equipment. She paused for a moment, savoring the crisp morning air. The town was still quiet, save for the distant crow of a rooster and the soft clopping of her boots on the wooden boardwalk.

As she approached the wagon she'd borrowed from Casper Jennings, her heart quickened with anticipation. She placed her camera and equipment next to the crate of dry plates, nestling them between blankets for the rough journey ahead.

Molly checked and double-checked her supplies, her fingers dancing over each item, as if performing a ritual. Satisfied everything was in order, she climbed onto the wagon seat and reached for the map Casper had drawn for her.

Unfolding the parchment, Molly studied the rough sketches and scribbled notes. Her gaze narrowed in concentration as she traced the path with her finger.

As she memorized the landmarks Casper had indicated, she felt a familiar thrill coursing through her veins. It was the same excitement that had driven her to leave Chicago, to seek out the untamed beauty of the West.

Molly folded the map and tucked it into her satchel. She gathered the reins, her hands steady despite the butterflies in her stomach.

As she urged the wagon forward, the first golden rays of sunlight crested the horizon, promising a day filled with beauty, challenges, and perhaps a touch of danger.

Little did Molly know just how prophetic the thought would prove to be.

As the sun climbed higher, Molly guided her wagon to a halt at the base of the mountains. The journey had been arduous, but the vista made every jolt and bump worthwhile. She climbed down from the wagon, her legs and back stiff from the ride.

"Oh, my. It's even more magnificent than I imagined."

She reached for the canteen and took a long, refreshing drink. The cool water was a balm to her parched throat. Settling herself on a nearby boulder, Molly retrieved the biscuits the hotel had packed for her.

As she ate, Molly's gaze roamed over the landscape. Towering peaks stretched toward the heavens, their snowcapped summits piercing the clouds. Lush forests cloaked the lower slopes, a tapestry of greens punctuated by the occasional flash of summer wildflowers.

She brushed the crumbs from her skirt and stood. There was work to be done, and the light wouldn't wait for her musings.

With practiced efficiency, Molly guided the wagon higher up the mountain trail. Each turn revealed new wonders, and she itched to capture them all. After another hour, she found the perfect spot. A plateau offering an unobstructed view of the valley below, and the majestic peaks above stretched before her.

Molly set about unloading her equipment. She'd

done this countless times before, but never in such a breathtaking location. As she assembled her camera, she found herself talking aloud, a habit born of long hours spent working alone.

"Now, let's see," she mused, adjusting the camera.

The world around her faded away, her entire focus narrowed to the view through her lens. Molly lost herself in her work, moving from one image to the next with single-minded determination.

As the sun arced across the sky, Molly continued to work. She didn't notice the passage of time, so engrossed in her art. The horses whinnied and danced around, but she ignored them. Only when she reached for another dry plate and discovered her supply was depleted did she realize how long she'd been at it.

Straightening, she looked around. Her eyes widened as she scanned the horizon, her heart suddenly racing. A massive plume of smoke billowed up from the base of the mountains, its dark tendrils reaching ominously toward the sky.

She gasped. "Fire!"

Panic threatened to overwhelm her for a moment before her innate survival instincts kicked in. With swift, decisive movements, she packed up her equipment. Her fingers flew over latches and straps, securing her precious camera and plates.

"Come on, come on," she muttered, glancing anxiously at the approaching smoke. The acrid scent was growing stronger by the second.

As she worked, she tried to form a plan, a way out.

The trail she'd taken up the mountain was likely already engulfed in flames. Her only option was to go higher, to find a safe haven above the fire line.

With the last of her gear stowed, Molly climbed onto the wagon. She grabbed, then slapped the reins, her knuckles white with tension.

The wagon lurched forward as she urged the horses up the steep incline. The path was treacherous, littered with loose rocks and deep ruts. Every jolt threatened to unseat her, but Molly clung on with grim determination.

"Just a little farther."

The heat at her back intensified, driving her onward. Sweat beaded on her brow, a mixture of exertion and fear. The smoke thickened, making it harder to see and breathe.

She coughed, her eyes watering. "Oh, Elijah," she whispered, her thoughts turning to the rugged rancher.

A loud crack split the air, followed by a thunderous crash. Molly whipped her head around to see a burning tree collapse across the path behind her.

She gasped, turning back to the trail ahead. "Just a bit more."

The wagon wheels caught on a deep rut, rocking the wagon into a precarious position. Her heart lodged in her throat as she fought to maintain control.

"No, no, no," she pleaded, and pulled hard on the reins.

Chapter Twenty-Two

The news of the wildfire spread through Mystic like a spark through dry tinder. Casper Jennings burst through the doors of the sheriff's office, his normally placid face etched with worry.

"Sheriff! It's Miss O'Sullivan. She's up in the mountains!"

Brodie Gaines looked up from his desk, his eyes narrowing. "What's this about Miss O'Sullivan?"

Casper leaned against the doorframe, panting. "The fire. It's raging at the base of the mountains. I gave her a map of the area. She rented a wagon and headed there this morning. She's up there, taking photographs."

Brodie stood, his chair almost toppling over in his haste. "You're certain?"

"As sure as I'm standing here." Casper nodded vigorously. "Said she wanted to capture the mountains before leaving for Helena."

Brodie's jaw clenched, his mind racing. "She's in real danger if the fire's as bad as I've been hearing."

"It is, Sheriff," Casper insisted. "I rode out toward the Beckett place. I've never seen anything like it. The smoke..." He shook his head.

Brodie grabbed his hat, striding toward the door. "I'm heading to Wild Spirit Ranch. Elijah needs to know."

As he mounted his horse, Brodie's thoughts turned to Molly. The spirited photographer had become a friend to many in Mystic, himself included. The idea of her alone, facing such danger, made his stomach churn.

"Hyah!" he called, spurring his horse into a gallop. The wind whipped at his face as he tore down the road toward Wild Spirit Ranch, each thundering hoofbeat matching the pounding of his heart.

"Hold on, Molly," he muttered. "We're coming for you."

Elijah Beckett stood in the yard of Wild Spirit Ranch, his gaze scanning the horizon as Brodie's urgent message sank in. Without hesitation, he turned to his brothers and the young cowboys gathered around him.

"Molly's out there," he said. "We need to move fast."

Cody, his older brother, stepped forward. "How do you want to do this, Eli?"

His mind began formulating a strategy. "We'll

split into three groups. Cody, you take the east slope with two of the hands. Joshua, you're with me on the central path. Nathan, take a group up the western trail with Parker and two more of the hands. The rest of the hands will stay here."

The men nodded, their faces grim with determination.

"What about us?" Annalee, his younger sister, called out, Lilian at her side.

Elijah shook his head. "You stay here. We need someone to prepare for when we bring her back."

"But—" Annalee started to protest.

"No arguments," Elijah cut her off, his tone brooking no dissent. "Time's wasting. Gear up, everyone. Bandanas, canteens, rope. We don't know what we're riding into."

As the group dispersed to gather supplies, Joshua approached Elijah. "You think we'll find her in time?"

Elijah's jaw clenched. "We have to." The thought of Molly, alone and in danger, made his chest tighten in a way he wasn't ready to examine.

Within minutes, the search party was mounted and ready. Elijah surveyed the men, his gaze steady. "Remember, the smoke will be thick. Stay together, watch each other's backs. If you find her, fire three shots in the air. Let's ride!"

The thundering of hooves filled the air as they set off, dust billowing behind them. As they approached the foothills, the acrid smell of smoke grew stronger, and dark clouds loomed ominously ahead.

Elijah's group pressed on, the terrain growing

steeper and more treacherous. Sweat beaded on his brow, not just from the increasing heat. "Molly!" he called out, his voice echoing off the rocks. "Molly O'Sullivan!"

Joshua coughed beside him, pulling his water-soaked bandana higher. "Eli, this smoke's getting worse. How much farther do you reckon we can go?"

Elijah's eyes narrowed, scanning the haze-shrouded landscape. "As far as it takes," he growled, urging his horse forward. "I'm not leaving without her."

A loud crack split the air. Elijah's horse reared, nearly throwing him.

"Look out!" Samuel, one of the young cowboys, yelled. A burning tree crashed down not far from them, sending embers flying and horses dancing to get away.

Elijah's voice remained steady. "Stay calm. We keep moving. Molly's counting on us."

As they pressed on, fighting through the smoke and dodging falling debris, Elijah couldn't shake the image of Molly's vibrant eyes, her determined smile. He'd never met a woman quite like her—infuriating and captivating in equal measure.

"Hold on, Molly," he muttered under his breath, sweat streaking down his face. "Just hold on."

A deafening crack of thunder shook the air, and suddenly, the heavens opened. Rain poured down in sheets, hissing as it met the smoldering earth. Elijah blinked against the onslaught, relief and urgency warring within him.

"Thank you, God," Joshua shouted over the downpour.

Elijah's gaze scanned the smoky terrain. The rain was a blessing, though it cut down the visibility.

"Spread out," he shouted.

They fanned out, calling Molly's name. Elijah's heart hammered inside his chest, knowing each second was critical to their search. Then, through a gap in the smoke, he spotted a flash of color.

"There!" he yelled, spurring his horse forward. As he drew closer, his breath caught in his throat. Molly lay motionless on the ground, her camera equipment scattered around her.

Elijah jumped off his horse, closing the distance in long strides at the same time Joshua fired off three shots. Elijah dropped to his knees beside her, gently turning her over.

"Molly," he said, his usual stoicism cracking. "Molly, can you hear me?"

She didn't respond, her face pale beneath the soot. Elijah pressed his fingers to her neck, exhaling sharply when he felt a pulse. He looked at Joshua. "She's alive. We need to get her down the mountain and to the ranch."

Without hesitation, Elijah scooped Molly into his arms. Her head lolled against his chest, and a fierce protectiveness surged through him.

"I've got you," he murmured, rising to his feet. Elijah handed her off to Joshua before mounting his horse and taking her back into his arms.

The descent was treacherous. Rain-slicked rocks

threatened to send them tumbling with each step. Elijah refused to slow down, knowing how urgent it was to get medical help.

"Careful, Eli," Joshua cautioned as Elijah navigated a particularly steep section.

Elijah didn't respond, his entire focus on the precious burden in his arms and his horse. He had complete confidence in Twitch, his sure-footed Appaloosa gelding. Molly stirred slightly, a moan escaping her lips.

"Stay with me," Elijah urged, his voice low and intense.

As they descended, the air began to clear.

"Almost there," he told her. "Hold on a little longer. I'm not letting you go." Reaching the base of the mountain, he shouted at Joshua. "I'm taking her to the ranch. Ride to town and get the doctor."

Without waiting for a response, he spurred Twitch into action. The horse responded as if sensing the gravity of the situation. They tore across the rain-soaked landscape, the world blurring around them.

His arms ached from holding her, but he refused to loosen his grip. Her head rested against his shoulder, and he could feel her shallow breaths against his neck.

"Stay with me, Molly."

As they raced toward Wild Spirit Ranch, his mind whirled with a mix of emotions he wasn't accustomed to dealing with. Fear, hope, and a fierce protectiveness warred within him.

"I should've known you'd go chasing one more

photograph," he said, a hint of exasperation in his voice. "Always pushing boundaries, aren't you?"

Twitch's hooves thundered across a wooden bridge spanning Moon River. The ranch was close now, and he urged his mount on, continuing to talk next to her ear.

"We're almost there. When you wake up, I've got a few things to say to you about running off into danger."

As the familiar buildings of the ranch came into view, he allowed himself a moment of relief. But he knew the real fight was still ahead.

Grayson burst out of the house as his brother reined to a stop. "Eli! Is she—"

"Alive." Elijah's urgent voice cut him off. "Joshua is riding for the doctor."

Grayson held out his arms. "Hand her down to me."

Elijah complied, then held out his arms again.

"You've done your share," Grayson said as he rushed up the steps. "I'll carry her inside."

Jolene appeared in the doorway, her eyes widening at the sight of Molly's limp form. "Bring her in, quickly! Take her into the downstairs guest room."

As Grayson placed Molly on the bed, Elijah found himself reluctant to let go. He stared down at her while Jolene checked her breathing and pulse.

"Eli," Jolene said softly, "she's running a temperature. Would you mind getting me a cool bowl of water and clean cloths?"

He hesitated, his gaze never leaving Molly's face.

"I can't—" he started, then swallowed hard. "I can't lose her, Jolene."

Jolene's expression softened. "I know. Go get what I need. Let me do what I can until the doctor arrives."

Elijah rushed from the room, his normally impassive face a mask of worry and frustration. Grabbing a bowl, he filled it with cool water, lifting a stack of clean cloths from a cabinet before returning. Setting everything down, he dipped a cloth in the water. Wringing it out, he handed it to Jolene.

"She's got soot in her lungs," Jolene murmured, wiping Molly's face with the damp cloth. "We need to prop her up, help her breathe easier."

As they worked to make Molly more comfortable, the sound of approaching hoofbeats echoed from outside. Elijah rushed out of the room to the front door, hope surging in his chest.

Chapter Twenty-Three

Elijah sat by Molly's bedside, her small hand engulfed in his calloused palm. He hummed a low, soothing tune, something his mother used to sing, and watched her sleep. Propped up with pillows, her breathing was still labored but steadier since Doctor Wainwright's last visit. Her fever-flushed face had receded to a healthier hue, though her eyes remained dull with exhaustion when open. Now, with her eyes closed, she looked almost peaceful.

A sudden, wrenching cough burst from Molly's chest, waking her with a start. She winced, clutching her ribs as Elijah helped her sit up.

"Breathe slow," he instructed, his voice a deep, calming anchor. "In and out, nice and easy."

She gasped for air, each breath a painful endeavor. Elijah poured a glass of water and held it to her lips. She sipped a little, then pushed it away, her hand lingering on his.

"Thank you," she rasped, her voice a shadow of its usual confident self. "For everything."

"You don't have to thank me," he said, releasing her hand gently and standing. "I'll get Ma. She'll mix the herbs."

She sank back against the pillows, closing her eyes. The heat from the fire, the acrid taste of smoke, the panic—all of it rushed back to her in vivid flashes. She remembered strong arms lifting her against his chest, the long ride on a horse.

Elijah returned with his mother, Naomi. As usual, she exuded innate confidence mixed with maternal warmth. She carried a small wooden bowl and pestle, the scent of crushed leaves rising in a fragrant cloud.

"How's our patient?" Naomi asked, though her eyes were already assessing Molly.

"Stubborn as ever." Molly managed a weak smile.

"That's a good sign." Naomi handed the bowl to Elijah and took Molly's hand. "This will taste awful, but it'll help. Doctor Wainwright knows his stuff."

Elijah held the bowl to Molly's lips. She hesitated, then drank the thick, green mixture in a single, desperate gulp. Her face contorted in disgust.

"Poison would be sweeter," she said, wiping her mouth with the back of her hand.

Naomi laughed. "If you can complain, you're on the mend. Now rest. We'll take care of everything." Naomi shot a look at her son before leaving the room while Elijah lingered.

"Elijah," Molly said, stopping him as he turned to go. "My equipment... and the wagon and horses..."

He paused, facing her. "Cody and a few men will head to the mountains tomorrow morning. The trail should be cooled off enough for them to search."

"Thank you. I know it's a lot to ask."

"It's no trouble. Don't worry about the horses. If they're on the mountain, Cody will find them."

She watched him leave, his broad shoulders filling the doorway, then turned her gaze to the ceiling. She didn't believe him, but it was nice to hear all the same.

The days passed with a slow, aching monotony. Molly's strength began to return, bit by bit. She started taking small steps around the room, then the hallway, always with someone from the Beckett clan nearby. Elijah was the most constant, though Jolene and Naomi made sure she was never alone.

On the fifth day, Grayson and Jolene entered the house after a trip to town, her face flushed with excitement. As usual, his features were unreadable. Molly was seated at the kitchen table, picking at a bowl of broth.

"We've retrieved your belongings," Jolene announced, holding up a familiar satchel. "And you'll never guess what we found."

Grayson held up a newspaper.

"You're famous." Jolene grinned.

Molly's eyes widened. "What is it?"

Grayson handed the paper to Jolene. "It's the Mystic Gazette," she said. "There's an article about you and your photographs. Says you're a pioneering artist who's documenting her westward journey."

Molly's heart quickened. "Let me see!"

Jolene held it just out of Molly's reach. "We

should wait for Elijah. He'll want to hear this."

Molly sank back in her chair, crossing her arms. "You lot are worse than my sisters."

Jolene shrugged, unrepentant. "We're a curious bunch."

Elijah walked in, wiping his hands on a rag. "What's all the yelling?"

Jolene thrust the newspaper at him. "Read this. It's about Molly."

He took the paper, his expression unreadable as he scanned the article. The room fell silent, all eyes on him. After a long moment, he looked up at Molly.

Molly's eyes burned with curiosity. "What is it? What does it say?"

Elijah cleared his throat, his gaze flickering over the newspaper before settling on Molly.

"Mystic's Unexpected Luminary: The Remarkable Miss O'Sullivan." A hint of a smile tugged at his lips.

Molly's eyes widened, her hand flying to her mouth. "Me? But…"

Elijah continued, his deep voice filling the room. "In an unexpected turn of events, our humble town of Mystic has found itself host to a rising star in the world of photography. Miss Molly O'Sullivan, whose breathtaking images of the American West have gained recognition in publications from Montana to Chicago."

He glanced up, noting the flush of color in Molly's cheeks. Her eyes sparkled with a mix of embarrassment and pride.

"There's more." Elijah's tone softened. "Miss

O'Sullivan's ability to blend the raw, untamed nature of the frontier with the growing civilization of the West showcases a talent beyond her years. What our readers recently learned was how Miss O'Sullivan narrowly escaped tragedy in a wildfire in Mystic Valley while photographing the magnificent landscape."

Molly sat in stunned silence. "I had no idea Faith planned to run an article about me and my work," she murmured.

Elijah folded the paper, his gaze lingering on her. "Seems you've made quite a name for yourself," he said, a note of respect in his voice. "You should be proud. It's a good article."

Two weeks passed, each day bringing Molly closer to full health. After supper one evening, as the sun began its slow descent, Elijah invited Molly to take a short walk with him.

"How are you feeling?" he asked, his eyes scanning the horizon out of habit.

Molly took a deep breath, thankful for the crisp mountain air. "Much better, thanks to you and your family."

Elijah offered a slow grin, a comfortable silence falling between them. After a moment, he spoke again. "Have you given any thought to your plans? Will you still be heading to Seattle?"

The question hung in the air, heavy with unspoken implications. Molly's steps faltered for a moment.

"Yes, I intend to continue to Seattle," she said, her voice firm. "But..." She hesitated, a flicker of vulnerability crossing her face. "I was hoping you might consider accompanying me."

Elijah's eyebrows shot up, surprise etched across his rugged features. He hadn't expected this independent woman to seek his company. "You want me to go with you?" he asked, his voice low and gravelly.

Molly nodded, a slight blush coloring her cheeks. "I've come to value your friendship, Elijah. And I think having a guide who knows the territory would be invaluable."

He considered the implications of her request. The ranch needed him, though not as much with Cody's return. The thought of traveling to Seattle with Molly stirred something deep within him. Grayson had seen much of the country, as had Cody.

Perhaps it was time for him to venture outside the ranch, bring back stories to entertain the family. He gazed out at the vast expanse of Mystic Valley, his internal struggle playing out across his face.

"I'll go." His gaze locked with hers. "Under one condition."

Molly tilted her head, curiosity piqued. "And what's that?"

Elijah took a deep breath, his heart pounding in his chest. "That you agree to marry me."

The words hung in the air between them, heavy with possibility and the promise of a future neither had anticipated when they first met.

Molly's eyes widened, her breath catching in her throat. For a moment, she stood frozen, the only sound the distant lowing of cattle and the gentle rustle of wind through the prairie grass.

"Marry you?" she finally managed, her voice barely above a whisper.

Elijah stepped closer. "I know it's sudden. These past weeks, getting to know you... they've changed everything. I love you, Molly. Your strength, your spirit, your kindness. I want to spend my life with you, if you'll have me."

His hand reached for hers, enveloping it in a gentle grip. Her heart beat an almost painful rhythm as she considered his words. She'd come to Montana seeking adventure and independence, not expecting to find love.

"Elijah, I..." she started, her voice trembling. "I never thought I'd want to marry. My photography, my career..."

"I'm not asking you to give anything up. I want to support your dreams while I'm free to fulfill mine. We'd be partners."

She searched his face, seeing the sincerity there. Memories of their time together flashed through her mind. His quiet strength during the fire, his unwavering support as she recovered, and the way he listened to her ideas with genuine interest had intensified the love she already held for him.

"I love you, too," she admitted, a smile breaking across her face. "Yes, Elijah Beckett. Yes, I'll marry you."

His usual restraint crumbled as he pulled her into a fierce embrace. Their lips met for a slow, tender kiss declaring their promise of a future together. When they pulled apart, Molly felt a warmth the cold night couldn't touch.

Epilogue

Three weeks later...

The tower bell rang out, filling the air with a joyous sound that mingled with the laughter and chatter of those gathered in the park behind the church. Elijah Beckett and Molly O'Sullivan stood side by side, hand in hand, surrounded by friends and family who'd witnessed their wedding ceremony. Her eyes sparkled with happiness, and she laughed as one of the guests made a teasing comment about her new husband's stern character.

"He's not as stern as you think," Molly assured, squeezing Elijah's hand. "Are you, love?"

Elijah allowed a small, reserved smile to play at the corners of his mouth. "If you say so."

Molly had come to understand he showed his softer side only when with family and close friends. Today should've been one of those occasions. Instead, he hid himself in a cloak of detachment, masking his emotions behind a veneer of composure, as if the joy surrounding them was too overwhelming to bear openly.

At the edge of the park, near the refreshment tables, Cody Beckett stood alone. He watched the festivities with a detached air, his ever-vigilant eyes taking in the scene without really seeing it. A few well-wishers approached him, and he greeted them with curt nods and brief handshakes. Each withdrew quickly, sensing Cody's desire for solitude.

His thoughts drifted to another wedding, years earlier, in this same church. He and Miriam had stood where Elijah and Molly were now, bathed in the same hopeful light. It was painful to remember how happy he'd been, how certain of the future. The memories of Miriam and Sophia were never far from his mind, and today, they gnawed at him with a particular ferocity.

He pushed the thoughts away, focusing instead on the ranch. With Elijah away, his brother's responsibilities would fall on Cody's shoulders. He welcomed the added chores. Work was the one thing that kept him from drowning in his grief, and he was grateful for its unending demands.

Cody's gaze wandered to the giant oak tree in the center of the park. A swing hung from one of its massive branches, where Joshua Beckett pushed Faith Goodell, the two of them laughing and talking like the children they once were. Faith's blonde hair streamed behind her as she shouted for Joshua to slow her down. After a moment, he complied, pushing her at a more relaxed pace.

"We're printing twice a week now," Faith said as

the swing made a lazy arc. "Circulation's doubled since spring."

Joshua smiled. "Sounds like the Bozeman Chronotype has some real competition."

"P.J. Bogart doesn't know what to do with himself," Faith said with a grin. "He's even offered me a job."

"Are you going to take it?"

"Of course not. The Bozeman Chronotype isn't the Mystic Gazette."

They lapsed into a comfortable silence, the kind formed over years of friendship. Joshua had always been quieter than most of the Beckett brothers. With Faith, he didn't need to speak much. She understood him in a way few others did.

"I'm excited for the articles and photographs Molly will be sending," Faith said after a while. "It'll be like she's writing a diary for us."

Joshua nodded. "She'll make a fine correspondent. And a finer sister-in-law."

A train whistle sounded in the distance, catching the attention of the crowd. It signaled the departure of Elijah and Molly, and the park began to empty as people made their way to the train station. There was a sense of unity in the procession, a communal desire to send the newlyweds off with the fullest measure of support.

At the station, Elijah and Molly took turns hugging their family and friends. Molly's eyes were bright with tears as she kissed Joshua on the cheek. "Take care of the family." She glanced at the group of

Becketts surrounding them.

"We will," Joshua assured her. "You two enjoy your travels."

Elijah shook Joshua's hand, then Cody's. "I'll be back before you know it."

Cody's face was a mask. "Just be sure to come back."

With that, Elijah and Molly boarded the train. It lurched forward, and the crowd waved and shouted their goodbyes. Elijah and Molly stood on the rear platform, hand in hand, waving until the train rounded a bend and disappeared from view.

The crowd began to disperse, trickling away in small groups. Joshua lingered, casting a glance at Faith, who stood on tiptoe to see if the train might come back into sight.

"Do you think they'll be happy?" she asked, turning to Joshua.

"They will," Joshua said. "Elijah loves her more than he knows how to say."

Faith nodded, then smiled. "Walk me home?"

Joshua's heart gave a small, hopeful leap. "Of course."

They started down the main street of Mystic, the town quiet with the end of the festivities. Most businesses were shuttered for the day, and the only sounds were the soft murmurs of those still making their way from the station.

"I always liked this time of day," Faith said. "Feels like the town is taking a deep breath."

Joshua laughed softly. "You mean, when it's not

bustling with news?"

"Bustling," she repeated with a chuckle. "Mystic's version of bustling is still a yawn for most places."

They walked in silence for a few moments, enjoying the peace. Joshua thought about the swing, about how he'd once pushed Faith just as high when they were children. He wondered when their friendship had become something more in his mind and whether she felt the same.

Thank you for reading **Wild Spirit Revival**, book one in the **Montana Becketts, Wild Spirit Ranch** historical western romance series.

The series prequel, Montana Bound Marshal, is available for free on My Webstore at **https://shirleendavies.com/product/montana-bound-marshal/**

If you enjoyed Wild Spirit Revival, here is another series you'll want to read: **Redemption Mountain**, a historical western romance series set in the turbulent era after the Civil War.

If you want to keep current on all my preorders, new releases, and other happenings, sign up for my Newsletter at **https://shirleendavies.com/shirleens-shop/**.

A Note from Shirleen

Thank you for taking the time to read **Wild Spirit Revival**!

If you enjoyed it, please consider telling your friends or posting a short review. Word of mouth is an author's best friend and is much appreciated.

I care about quality, so if you find something in error, please contact me via email at **shirleen@shirleendavies.com**

Books by Shirleen Davies

Contemporary Western Romance Series

Macklins of Whiskey Bend

Thorn
Del
Boone
Kell
Zane

Cowboys of Whistle Rock Ranch

The Cowboy's Road Home, Book One
The Cowboy's False Start, Book Two
The Cowboy's Second Chance Family, Book Three
The Cowboy's Final Ride, Book Four
The Cowboy's Surprise Reunion, Book Five
The Cowboy's Counterfeit Fiancée, Book Six
The Cowboy's Ultimate Challenge, Book Seven
The Cowboy's Simple Solution, Book Eight
The Cowboy's Broken Dream, Book Nine
The Cowboy's Leap of Faith, Book Ten
A Cowboy Christmas at Whistle Rock Ranch, Book Eleven
The Cowboy's Change of Heart, Book Twelve, Coming Next in the Series!

MacLarens of Fire Mountain

Second Summer, Book One
Hard Landing, Book Two
One More Day, Book Three
All Your Nights, Book Four
Always Love You, Book Five
Hearts Don't Lie, Book Six
No Getting Over You, Book Seven
'Til the Sun Comes Up, Book Eight
Foolish Heart, Book Nine

Historical Western Romance Series

Redemption Mountain

Redemption's Edge, Book One
Wildfire Creek, Book Two
Sunrise Ridge, Book Three
Dixie Moon, Book Four
Survivor Pass, Book Five
Promise Trail, Book Six
Deep River, Book Seven
Courage Canyon, Book Eight
Forsaken Falls, Book Nine
Solitude Gorge, Book Ten
Rogue Rapids, Book Eleven
Angel Peak, Book Twelve
Restless Wind, Book Thirteen
Storm Summit, Book Fourteen

Mystery Mesa, Book Fifteen
Thunder Valley, Book Sixteen
A Very Splendor Christmas, Holiday Novella, Book Seventeen
Paradise Point, Book Eighteen
Silent Sunset, Book Nineteen
Rocky Basin, Book Twenty
Captive Dawn, Book Twenty-One
Whisper Lake, Another Very Splendor Christmas, Book Twenty-Two
Mustang Meadow, Book Twenty-Three
Solitary Glen, Book Twenty-Four
Ghost Lagoon, Book Twenty-Five
Renegade Woods, Book Twenty-Six
A Redemption Mountain Christmas, Book Twenty-Seven
Hidden Horizon, Book Twenty-Eight, Coming Next in the Series!

Montana Becketts ♦ Wild Spirit Ranch

Montana Bound Marshal, Prequel
Wild Spirit Revival, Book One
Heart of Mystic Valley, Book Two
Storm in Montana, Book Three, Coming Next in the Series!

MacLarens of Fire Mountain

Tougher than the Rest, Book One
Faster than the Rest, Book Two
Harder than the Rest, Book Three

Stronger than the Rest, Book Four
Deadlier than the Rest, Book Five
Wilder than the Rest, Book Six

MacLarens of Boundary Mountain

Colin's Quest, Book One,
Brodie's Gamble, Book Two
Quinn's Honor, Book Three
Sam's Legacy, Book Four
Heather's Choice, Book Five
Nate's Destiny, Book Six
Blaine's Wager, Book Seven
Fletcher's Pride, Book Eight
Bay's Desire, Book Nine
Cam's Hope, Book Ten

Romantic Suspense

Eternal Brethren Military Romantic Suspense

Steadfast, Book One
Shattered, Book Two
Haunted, Book Three
Untamed, Book Four
Devoted, Book Five
Faithful, Book Six
Exposed, Book Seven
Undaunted, Book Eight

Resolute, Book Nine
Unspoken, Book Ten
Defiant, Book Eleven

Peregrine Bay Romantic Suspense

Reclaiming Love, Book One
Our Kind of Love, Book Two

Find all of my books at:
www.shirleendavies.com/books.html

About Shirleen

Shirleen Davies writes romance—historical and contemporary western romance, and romantic suspense. She grew up in Southern California, attended Oregon State University, and has degrees from San Diego State University and the University of Maryland. During the day, she provides consulting services to small and mid-sized businesses. But her real passion is writing emotionally charged stories of flawed people who find redemption through love and acceptance. She now lives with her husband in a beautiful town in northern Arizona.

I love to hear from my readers!
Send me an email: shirleen@shirleendavies.com
Visit my Website: www.shirleendavies.com
Sign up to be notified of New Releases:
www.shirleendavies.com/contact
Follow me on Amazon:
amazon.com/author/shirleendavies
Follow me on BookBub:
bookbub.com/authors/shirleen-davies

Other ways to connect with me:
Facebook Author Page:
facebook.com/shirleendaviesauthor
Pinterest: pinterest.com/shirleendavies
Instagram: instagram.com/shirleendavies_author
TikTok: shirleendavies_author
Twitter: www.twitter.com/shirleendavies

Copyright © 2024 by Shirleen Davies

All rights reserved. No part of this publication may be reproduced, distributed, or transmitted in any form or by any electronic or mechanical means, including information storage and retrieval systems or transmitted in any form or by any means without the prior written permission of the publisher, except by a reviewer who may quote brief passages in a review. No AI Training. Without in any way limiting the author's exclusive rights under copyright, any use of this publication to 'train' artificial intelligence (AI) technologies to generate text is expressly prohibited. The author reserves all rights to license uses of this work for generative AI training and development of machine learning language models. Thank you for respecting the hard work of this author.

> For permission requests, contact the publisher.
> Avalanche Ranch Press, LLC
> PO Box 12618
> Prescott, AZ 86304

Wild Spirit Revival is a work of fiction. Names, characters, places, and incidents are either products of the author's imagination or used fictitiously. Any resemblance to actual events, locales, or persons, living or dead, is wholly coincidental.

Printed in Great Britain
by Amazon